A
SHORT TALE
OF
SHAME

ANGEL IGOV

A
SHORT TALE
OF
SHAME

TRANSLATED FROM
THE BULGARIAN BY
ANGELA RODEL

OPEN LETTER
LITERARY TRANSLATIONS FROM THE UNIVERSITY OF ROCHESTER

This book was written at the creative centers IWTC in Rhodes, Greece, and at Hostel Situla in Novo Mesto, Slovenia, thanks to the international program Halma.

Library of Congress Cataloging-in-Publication Data: Available upon request.
ISBN-13: 978-1-934824-76-4 / ISBN-10: 1-934824-76-3

This book is published within the Elizabeth Kostova Foundation's program for Support of Contemporary Bulgarian Writers and in collaboration with the America for Bulgaria Foundation.

Elizabeth Kostova
FOUNDATION *for*
CREATIVE WRITING

AMERICA FOR BULGARIA
F O U N D A T I O N
Фондация Америка за България

Printed on acid-free paper in the United States of America.

Text set in Dante, a mid-20th-century book typeface designed by Giovanni Mardersteig. The original type was cut by Charles Malin.

Design by N. J. Furl

Open Letter is the University of Rochester's nonprofit, literary translation press: Lattimore Hall 411, Box 270082, Rochester, NY 14627

www.openletterbooks.org

[1] The girl next to him fell silent and it took Krustev a while to realize that she had fallen asleep. He looked in the rear-view mirror: the other two kids were also dozing in the back seat. He himself had hardly slept the last few nights and longed to feel drowsy. Since the middle of April he had been suffering from insomnia more and more frequently. He refused to take pills; he put on his jacket, went out into the garden, and stared at the patterns on the birch trees for hours. They were perfect in their spontaneity.

The noonday sun made people sleepy and insects crazy. Krustev was driving quickly and from time to time a black fly would hit the windshield with a dull thud. There was a fly, now there's not. Period. I'm surrounded by sleepers, Krustev said to himself. Instead of envy, he felt claustrophobia: the teenagers' triune sleep pulsated in rhythm with their deep breathing, each breath filling the car to its utmost limits and pressing Krustev to the wheel—a fluffy, shapeless white mass, receding and swelling again, a sea of sleep, a white sea, the Aegean, they were traveling towards it, yet it had already slipped into their car.

The phone of the girl next to him buzzed like a fly: *Hello, I love you, won't you tell me your name*, so they listen to '60s music. Krustev felt flattered, as if he had written the song. He hadn't written it, but he had played it in one of his wilder bands back in the day, which was called Stinkweed—archeologists had just discovered the ancient sanctuary near the village of Stinkweed, shades of pagan priests and memory-weary stones. The singer, for his part, chewed stinkweed and spent whole days in the kingdom of the shades. The band didn't last long.

The girl stirred, dug her phone out of her cargo pants and rasped: Hello? She explained that she couldn't go wherever they were inviting her because she was on her way to the Aegean Sea. The other end of the line was apparently envious. The date was put off for some other awakening. Krustev didn't start a conversation with her. He could sense her clumsily cleaning off the sleep that had clung to her so strongly precisely because it had been so short. The girl sighed and rubbed her eyes.

I know you, she said suddenly. Me? You. You're Elena's dad. Krustev let out a laugh, only later would he realize how long it had been since that had happened. I can't deny it, he said, and who are you? Maya. I've known Elena since we were kids. Do you remember me?

Maya. A fleeting memory of a studious little blonde girl who perhaps sat next to his daughter in elementary school carelessly flitted through Krustev's mind. The young woman now sitting on the other side of the stick shift was also blonde, but she didn't look too studious. Maya. I think I do remember you, Krustev said. We went to the same grade school, Maya continued, then we lost touch, but then we found each other again. It was really funny, because both of us had changed so much that it was like we were meeting again for the first time. But we liked each other again. She's in America now, Krustev said. I know, said Maya, we used to see each other pretty often before she left, once she had a party at your place and I saw your picture there, otherwise I wouldn't have recognized you. Krustev mentally noted the compliment. The family picture which hung in a frame in the living room was taken five years ago. He had been only twenty-five when his daughter was born. She was now twenty, so that meant that's how old the girl next to him was. Sometimes it occurred to him that he was getting old, just as it occurs to you that you've forgotten to call an old acquaintance whom you ran into on the street and promised to call. He rubbed his stubbly face with his palm. Have you kept in touch since she's been there? Actually, no, Maya said, she's somehow dropped off the radar. Or maybe I have. Krustev could smell some kind of intrigue, but he left it for later, he had fired off his questions solely to find out whether the girl knew something of *the events in his family,* that's how various concerned relatives and business partners, whose repulsively soft and sweaty hands reached out to squeeze him in insipid sympathy, put it, but since she hadn't been in touch with Elena, most likely she didn't know. He was tired of everyone knowing. That's why he'd taken off in his car. The trees along the roadside didn't know.

It hadn't even crossed his mind to pick up hitchhikers along the way, in fact, he had hardly seen any hitchhikers in recent years;

the person who until recently had hitchhiked either now had a car or had left for somewhere much further away, like his daughter. She had hitched a lot in high school, that is, her official stories always said otherwise, but Krustev and her mother could tell, they worried, but kept quiet, after all, they were young enough to remember the stunts they had pulled at her age. Only Elena seemed not to know that they knew she hitchhiked, and for quite some time Krustev wondered what the point of this secrecy was, but afterwards decided that his daughter simply needed to keep secrets from her parents and while it had seemed laughable to him at first, later he accepted it as normal. Over the past few years, however, hitchhikers had become few and far between, most often foreign couples with huge backpacks, with skin tanned and hair bleached by the sun, sometimes he stopped for them, just for some company, but their stories inevitably turned out to be identical, the stories of young, curious Europeans wading into the weed patch of Balkan exoticism, and he had almost stopped picking people up, he only did it when some completely sudden impulse whispered to him and in those cases he never regretted it. Now that same impulse had stopped him in that place, the first straight stretch since he had entered the mountains, and he was surprised that such a place even existed, a long sigh in the road before the next bend. There were three of them. The other girl and the young man were still dozing in the back seat and Krustev suspected they had also seen his picture in the living room. He felt a slightly unpleasant tickle: he was driving strangers who had been in his house and had probably even properly trashed it, as usually happened at Elena's parties. But perhaps they were his stroke of luck, they had a destination, they wanted to reach Thasos. He envied them. He had simply gathered up some luggage, checked his credit cards, and taken off in the car just like that, to wherever he felt like. And when he had stopped for them, and they had asked where he was headed, he had frankly admitted that he didn't know, it hadn't crossed his mind the whole morning that he didn't know where he was going. Now this is what I call hitching, the black-haired girl declared, as she settled into the back seat. He jammed their backpacks into the trunk and said since they were going to Thasos, he would drive them to the port at Datum, but he didn't think—it only fleetingly occurred to him—why shouldn't he, too, continue on to the island by ferryboat, maybe even along with them, he didn't so much need the company—he needed to know where he was going. Did this make him a tagalong, but hey, they were the ones who had gotten into his car.

So, Maya piped up, why did you just take off in your car? Krustev was silent for a moment, then replied why not? That's great, if you can get away with it, the girl murmured, Krustev grunted. I guess I didn't have a choice, he said, but I'll explain it to you later. She kept quiet. She was surely looking at him in confusion, but he avoided her gaze and stared at the road. What should he say now? Fortunately, the backseat came to life, hey, we actually fell asleep, the young man yawned. You know who's driving us, Maya turned to him. Elena's dad. Boril Krustev.

Krustev almost never heard his full name these days. When he was young, he had liked stating it in a defiant tone, it uncompromisingly drove home his Slavic descent, and in the '80s that could stir up trouble for you in the capital, but Krustev had learned to wield it like a sword, a cold weapon which drew blood. Afterwards, of course, things had settled down, at the moment being a Slav in Thrace was no worse than being an Illyrian or Paeonian, and it was definitely much better than being a Dacian. Since the accepted wisdom back then was that Slavs could either work the fields or sing mournful songs, Krustev left the fields to his grandfather and started playing, his music grew ever less mournful and they even became stars of sorts, and later it was no longer so important whether you were a Slav and after he left his last and most successful group, everything had worked out amazingly easily for him, the promotion agency, the big concerts, and the stores for audio-visual equipment alongside that, he had become comfortably wealthy and it was as if this made him less of a Slav, or people just didn't care so much about that now, and he didn't care, either.

The young man was worked up about something else, however, since he was Boril Krustev, was he playing anywhere these days? No, only for fun, and even then rarely, Krustev said, skipping over the fact that that, too, had not happened to him in a long time, he hadn't played in public for ten years now, since Euphoria had broken up. Then everyone from the group had set out on their own paths and all those paths led equally far from music, towards the world of private business, which had opened up with liberal aplomb, from the very beginning Krustev had decided that he would bring foreign bands to play in Thrace and wouldn't you know, it had worked out; sometimes, going back over his memories, it positively spooked him to think how badly he had wanted to break into that business without any cash, with only his love of music and the connections he had made abroad, and how quickly everything had taken off, those were crazy times, he would tell himself, crazy times. The young man really liked Euphoria, however, especially the first album, and hinted that they could get back together at some point, isn't that what usually happens, the dinosaurs of rock suddenly get back together and go on tour. Krustev chuckled despite himself. So they already counted him as a dinosaur. This was getting more fun by the minute, he had done right in picking them up. The young man kept chattering on about Euphoria and Krustev was thankful that he didn't mention his daughter at all, even though he knew that it would come up at some point, but didn't he miss the rock-and-roll lifestyle sometimes? Krustev started to explain that when he had been his age (he mentally smacked himself for the expression) he was just getting into those things and they had seemed so romantic to him, music, freedom, being on the road, people loving you, getting into you, and playing like crazy; but there's also the flipside of the coin, all the slogging, exhaustion, alcohol, drugs and fights of every kind, because you've teamed up with people who all think that they're the shit, believe me, Krustev said, if I could turn back time, I'd spare myself at least half of all that. He inhaled more noisily than he meant to. He hadn't strung so many sentences together for months and he wasn't even sure it was sincere, actually he was sure that it wasn't sincere, but he badly needed to reject his entire past, especially now, to transform himself merely into the person behind the wheel, with no history, no life and no death, a function of the highway, the mileage. So, he's a pureblooded Thracian, probably of communist stock at that. You're not a musician, are you, Spartacus? Well, no, actually, it doesn't really go with his name, the black-haired girl suddenly chimed in, I mean, if he'd been Orpheus . . . Since Sirma's also awake, our little clique is now at full strength, Maya said next to him. I've been awake for a long time, if you really want to know, I was listening to you and thinking about various things; Sirma, nice to meet you, she moved so that Krustev could see her in the mirror, curly black hair and blue eyes, and waved at him. So you're Elena's dad. Talk about crazy. Now that's what I call a coincidence. It's not fair, Krustev tried to joke, you all know my daughter, you also know me vicariously, but I don't know anything about you. There's time, Sirma yawned, didn't you say you don't know where you're going? Krustev really didn't know where he was going and Sirma suggested point-blank that he come with them. It makes sense, he thought, that way they have a sure ride, they don't seem the type to lounge around frying on the beaches of Thasos for more than a day or two. However, they hadn't decided where to go after that. Maya laughed nervously, she had also thought of asking him to come along, but you know how she is, while she was sitting there wondering how to put it, Sirma had beat her to it. Sirma was clearly the boss and Krustev asked her if they wouldn't get annoyed with an old fart like him. Again he told himself that he shouldn't talk about what was coming up, don't act with them like everybody your age acts with them, drop the Elena's dad act. But he wasn't sure he could put on any other act. Maya and Spartacus burst into energetic protest, talking over each other. Sirma waited for their buzzing to die down and simply said, come on now, in a businesslike tone.

And with that, things likely should have been considered decided.

In the house, the windows are sleeping, the furniture is sleeping, the refrigerator is sleeping, a plug dangling from its shoulder. The doors are sleeping: beautiful, solid, heavy doors. Krustev is sleeping, hung on the wall, his wife is sleeping on one side of him, his daughter on the other, they are sleeping with open eyes, smiling amid the garden outside. The empty bottles jammed into the black bag in the hallway are sleeping. The air conditioner. The lawnmower. The dirty dishes piled in the dishwasher. The slippers, collapsed from exhaustion, are sleeping in indecent poses.

Sssssleep . . . The only ones standing guard are the tiny lights of the alarm system and a few inexperienced spiders, who have stretched their webs in various corners of various rooms, stalking their puny prey, without an inkling of one another's existence.

As if to make up for this, the whole garden is awake: the birch trees are whispering, the willow is murmuring incomprehensibly, in the furrows the multifarious plants with Latin names are trying out their new flowers and buzzing excitedly in exotic languages, the rock garden is juggling miniature stones and there, next to it, on the lawn, is the place where their family picture was taken five years ago, the places where the three of them have set foot can be clearly seen, where they carved the moment in gently and unrelentingly, there the grass is flattened and will not straighten up again.

Actually, it suddenly popped into Krustev's mind, aren't these three in college? It's the middle of May, shouldn't they be going to lectures right now? He received a full-on lecture in reply. All three of us are taking time off, Maya explained. At the end of sophomore year, lots of people begin doubting whether their major is really for them, they had, too. The three of them had gotten together at the end of last summer and decided that they would give themselves a year to clear things up, then they would decide whether to keep the same majors or to change, interesting, Krustev said, do the three of you always decide what to do as a group? Pretty often, the girl again gave her nervous laugh. It's been like that since the beginning of high school, always the three of us together. In the beginning everybody thought it was weird, Spartacus cut in, then little by little they got used to it, at the end of the day there are people with much stranger relationships. Krustev couldn't disagree with that, he himself handled strange relationships well, significantly more successfully than normal ones, take me, for example, Spartacus continued, I'm in law school. Sirma jokes that that's why I'm such a chatterbox. Right now, I can't say that I don't want to study law anymore. It's just that I need a year off to think things over and figure out whether I really want to go into law or if I'd rather do something else, and now's the time, because afterwards it will be too late . . . Sirma wanted to know what Krustev's major had been. Me? He had studied management. Only it was different then, he shrugged, I never really had the college experience, because of music I started my BA a lot later, after the Euphoria guys and I had ditched our instruments and decided to go into business. And I was in a hurry to graduate, even though I'm sure it would've been the same, even without a diploma. While they were teaching me how to run a company, I was already running three. He suddenly thought this sounded too arrogant and added that in those years, that happened a lot, it still does now, too, Maya said.

The road rushed on ahead and took the curves fast, narrow, but nice, repaved recently with the Union's money, traffic was light, few drivers chose to pass through the heart of the Rhodopes on their way to the sea, and Krustev felt a fleeting, hesitant delight in the freedom to drive freely, without getting furious over the trucks and junkers blocking traffic. Below them, to the left, was the river, high since all the snow had already melted, running its course with a cold and no-nonsense determination; beyond it rippled the newly greened hills. They passed through several villages, long and narrow, built along the river, with two-story houses, their black wooden timbers sternly crossed over whitewashed walls. Since few cars passed, people were walking along the highway here and there, sinewy grandfathers and ancient grandmothers, some even leading goats and from the backseat Sirma for no rhyme or reason announced that she had dreamed of being a goat her whole life, but didn't manage to expand on her argument, seemingly having dozed off again. Krustev put on some music, Maya and Spartacus, perhaps to make him happy, or perhaps completely spontaneously, sang along quietly and swayed in rhythm such that in their interpretation, the careless rock, designed for Saturday night and chicks in leather jackets, sounded and looked like some mystical Indian mantra. Krustev kept silent, he drove slowly through the villages and looked at the people. They spontaneously reminded him of his grandfather, a strange, scowling person, who always looked angry before you started talking to him, then it turned out that he gladly gave himself over to shooting the breeze and telling stories, mostly amusing tales, one, however, the most recent story, was swollen with darkness and violence, and Krustev thought of it from time to time. His grandfather's village lay on the border of the Ludogorie region, the only Slavic village around, and his house was on the very edge of the village, near the river, a quiet village, pleasant, albeit a lost cause, the communists had forgotten it in their general industrialization, occupied as they were with the more densely Slavic regions, after the fall of communism the state had left the Slavs in peace once and for all, but back then it was the Dacians' turn, they had moved into erstwhile Thracian towns, and, of course, in the end they fought, the Thracians called it "The Three Months of Unrest," while everyone else called it the Civil War of '73. Before the war, everyone from my grandfather's village figured that the quarrels between the Thracians and the Dacians weren't their business, they even joked about how the names of the two peoples rhymed, people for whom they felt equally little love lost, the civil war in the Ludogorie, however, made the hostility their business, too. The battles began, the Dacian militias defended their cities street by street and building by building against the army, who rolled in with tanks, but the tanks didn't do much good in a war in which you couldn't see your enemy. Everything really had lasted only three months and Krustev, no matter how young he had been then, could confirm that beyond the region and even in the capital, people were hardly aware of the unrest in practice, his father and mother said the same thing, his grandfather's village, however, was a whole different story. For three days they heard machine gun fire from the direction of the city, all the radios were turned on in hopes of picking up some news, but they only played cheerful Thracian music around the clock. On the third day, the shooting ceased. A rumor spread that the army had taken the city and that the Dacian fighters had scattered, every man trying to save his own skin however he could. The village mayor warned them not to take any Dacians into their homes, should they arrive. Only five years had passed since the Slavic events in Moesia and everyone was afraid of what might happen if Thracian soldiers came to search the village and found hidden enemy fighters. That evening, my grandfather went out to feed his animals and when he opened the door of the barn, he saw two human eyes. It was a young man, no older than twenty, with dirty, matted hair, a gashed forehead and blood stains on his ragged striped shirt, like the shirts the Dacian militias had worn, he hadn't even managed to take it off. He was severely wounded and feverish, wheezing, rolling his eyes from the cow to the mule and back again, he didn't say anything. What could Krustev's grandfather do? All alone in the very last house, just as his village was all alone between the hammer and the anvil of this war, which was not its own. Perhaps the boy would die before the soldiers came, but perhaps not. He left the barn, grabbed his hoe, went back in and brought it down on the boy's head with all the geezerly strength left in him. He loaded him on the mule somehow or other and threw him into the river. The neighbors kept quiet. The next day a Thracian regiment really did arrive in the village, searched a few houses, sniffed around suspiciously, doled out slaps to a few young men whose looks they didn't like, and went on their way. The river carried the corpse away and no one in the village mentioned it, his grandfather, however, for some unclear reason was sure that the neighbors had seen everything, he crossed himself surreptitiously, like under communism, and kept repeating, a terrible sin, a terrible sin, a terrible sin, but what else could I do? He lived a long life. He had told Krustev this story the same year that Elena was born and several months before he died. Much time had already passed, he had taken a second wife, a widow from the village, and he had continued living in the last house by the river. Senility was already getting the best of him and Krustev had even wondered whether he hadn't made the whole story up, because who, really, who could imagine his grandfather killing someone in cold blood with a hoe? Yes, indeed, he had lived in a different time, he had fought in two wars and had won medals for bravery, so that means he surely had killed people, but not with a hoe and not in his very own barn, although do the place and the method really change anything, Krustev grunted and tried to keep his mind on the road.

Sirma announced her latest awakening with a powerful yawn and a quick commentary on her friends' mantra-like chanting, and for the next half hour they all talked over one another, including Krustev. The asphalt was much better than on the last road. Maya, for her part, had never come this way. They argued for some time about whether she really hadn't. Krustev asked them whether they hitchhiked often. Not very often, they had done it more in high school. Surely his daughter had tagged along with them as well, but in any case, his observations about the decline of hitch-hiking were confirmed. The three of them generally tried to hitch together, sometimes they tried other combinations, but it never went as well. Spartacus had once hitched with three other guys and only a Gypsy horse cart had deigned to drive them between two villages, after which they split up, otherwise it was never going to work. Sirma, for her part, had hitched alone a couple times. Didn't you ever run into any trouble? No, only once, when a woman had picked her up. Everyone laughed at that, even Krustev. He was feeling better and better, he was tempted to say *more normal*, but he was no longer sure whether this was normal or whether, on the contrary, the scowling pre-dawn, semi-twilight he had inhab-ited for such a long time was. There had been flashes during the winter, too, but then Elena had left and he had collapsed again, only he didn't turn on the television, but read instead, first he read the books he had been given on various occasions in recent years, then the ones Elena had left in her room, after that he went to an online bookstore and ordered a whole series of contemporary titles in translation, they were delivered by van, an astonished young man unloaded two full cardboard boxes in his hallway and left, shaking his head pensively, Krustev read them, some were good, others not so good, but once he had closed the last one—a novel by a Dutch writer about a malicious, blind cellist—he decided that he wouldn't read anymore and that he had to get out of the house. Maya said that she thought she had forgotten her bathing suit. As if we haven't seen you without your bathing suit on, Spartacus replied, then realized that they weren't alone and fell silent, embar-rassed. The three of them seemed to spend so much time together that when they found themselves with other people, they quickly forgot about the others' presence. With the involuntary habit of the male imagination, Krustev envisioned the girl sitting next to him without her bathing suit for an instant and felt uncomfortable about it, as if he had made her an indecent proposal. She was his daughter's age. Sirma preferred Samothrace to Thasos. *Samo-thrace*, only Thracians, Krustev joked, without knowing whether they spoke Slavic, but at least Sirma seemed to get it and repeated in delight: Only Thracians, how cool is that! Thasos and Samothrace, the two islands the new state had managed to save when the Macedonian legacy was divvied up. Like many other Slavs, Krustev, with a nostalgia instilled by foreign books, sometimes dreamed of Macedonian times, when the Slavs were merely one of the dozens of people who had inhabited the empire and were in no case so special that they should be subjected to attempts at assimilation, but still, things were clearly changing. Twenty years ago, Thracian kids wouldn't have taken a ride from a Slav. Twenty years ago, there weren't many Slavs with their own cars and even fewer of them would have dared to drive straight through the Rhodopes. Had they been to any other Aegean islands? Last year the three of them had made it to Lemnos, while Maya had gone to Santorini with her father. We also want to go to Lesbos, Sirma announced. You two go right on ahead to Lesbos, Spartacus said, that island doesn't interest me a bit, they all burst out laughing. Krustev was impressed, however. So now that's possible, he said. We're all part of the Union and the borders are open. Do you know how hard it was to get a Phrygian visa back in the day? Especially for me, Sirma suddenly blurted out, seeing as how my grandfather is Lydian. But she had never set foot in Lydia. Spartacus and Maya looked extremely surprised, apparently not so much at her parentage, rather at the fact that there was something about her that they didn't know. The mood crashed for a whole five minutes, at which point Spartacus started talking about Euphoria's first album again, asking Krustev whether he had it with him in the car and insisting on putting it on. Later, Krustev replied, because in disbelieving gratitude for this kind-hearted twist of fate, he felt himself wanting to sleep, the curves ahead were giving off warm sleep, and when on the outskirts of the next village he saw a shabby roadside dive, he stopped immediately to drink a coffee.

[2]

What crazy good luck—to get picked up by someone who can drive them wherever they want to go, and he's not just some jerk, but Elena's dad! If she hadn't been sitting, Maya would've jumped for joy. When I get home, I'm gonna sit down and write her an email. Now here's a good reason, it was stupid of them not to write, to avoid each other because of some childish stunts from two whole years ago. Elena's dad looked like her—with ash-blond hair and a round Slavic face, whose features were perhaps too soft for a man, but which for that reason lent it a pleasant warmth, dignifying the otherwise severe nose and habitually pursed lips. It was strange, of course, to take off in your car just like that, aimlessly, on a long drive, that's what he told them, and a couple times he seemed to hint at some problems, indeed, he didn't look at all like a happy person, maybe it has something to do with Elena, she often created problems, why lie, although it could also have something to do with his wife, his health, his business. Maya wondered how rich he was. The car—she couldn't see the make, and she didn't know anything about cars anyway—was big, nice, comfortable, it drove smoothly but did not look luxurious by any stretch of the imagination. Elena, at least back then, hadn't had a lot of money. But their house was positively mind-blowing: spacious, light, opening out onto a huge garden, where she had met Dobrin at one of Elena's parties, lots of Elena's friends were Slavs and that surely made sense at the end of the day, and Dobrin in particular was really a good guy, fully in keeping with his name, which meant "good" in Slavic, but, of course, nothing lasts forever. And Boril Krustev was surely rich, but he didn't like showing it off with luxury and that definitely spoke well of him. How old was he? He looked young, definitely younger than her own father, with an almost athletic build, in fact, with a clean conscience you could say he was a good-looking man, yes, Elena was also pretty, a little too pretty, and she had been ever since she was a kid. Maya stared at the man's hands on the wheel, despite the fact that he was relatively husky, his fingers were rather delicate, a musician's fingers, after all, she told herself, even though B.B. King played divinely with his fat little sausages.

So Sirma was of Lydian descent. Maya couldn't have been more surprised if Sirma had suddenly mentioned casually that Sirma wasn't her real name, but instead something entirely different. Because her Lydian descent wasn't what mattered here, but the absurd fact that Sirma hadn't talked about it during all the years they had known one another, not only known one another, but had become a common organism, the three of them with Spartacus. It's like your right leg blurting out to your left hand something it had never suspected, hmm, maybe that isn't the best comparison, but given that it was something that wasn't important in the least, why hadn't she mentioned it until now? Was this some sort of secret, which had broken the skin that had concealed it suddenly and without resistance? In that case, Maya likely would have taken it better, she would've acknowledged her friend's right to have secrets, things she didn't want to talk about; but to keep quiet about something *that didn't matter*, that wasn't OK, because it puts you in a privileged position and Maya was taken aback by the whole pointlessness of the miscarried secret.

Elena's dad picked exactly that moment in her thoughts to ask how the three of them had met. They had met on the first day of high school, so it had been almost seven years now, which wasn't such a short time at all. Maya remembered very well how, curious, flustered and slightly scared, she had gone into the yard of her new school, a wide paved space swarming with unfamiliar faces, buzzing with unfamiliar voices—nobody here knew what they were in for, nobody knew what their class would be like, whether they'd make friends quickly, nobody knew who they'd end up sharing a desk with, who would be peeking into their notebook and whether that desk-mate would reek like garlic, here there were no long-standing desk-mates, everyone—OK, fine, with a few minor exceptions, but that only confirmed the rule—everyone was a stranger, everything was new for everyone, and everything had to start from the beginning, the first day of school was the first day of the world. Maya was convinced that she would screw something up and later it turned out that she really had screwed something up: she had gone to the wrong line, right next to the one her future class was forming, the faces in both lines were equally unfamiliar and there was no way to recognize her mistake, she timidly started talking to the girl next to her, who looked extremely bored with the welcoming ceremony, she wasn't carrying a backpack, but a canvas army-surplus bag like soldiers used, and actually she looked quite sketchy to Maya, but still she had to shoot the breeze with someone, and it turns out that was Sirma. Maya realized her mistake only when the classes started off towards their respective homerooms, so that *the rabbits* could introduce themselves to one another in peace, then she saw that 8-IV was written above the door her line was going into, and not 8-III, this was an additional muddle on top of everything else; this year the Ministry was instituting some reform which nobody understood, but in any case, the preparatory classes at the language high schools would now be called "eighth grade," and in contrast to the already-existing eighth grade classes, which had been preparatory the previous year, they would be divided up not by letters, but by Roman numerals, such that the chaos was total: if they asked you what grade you were in, you could no longer just say "eighth," you had to explain whether you were from the letter ones or the numeral ones, the latter, of course, were younger, and in the end the upper grades thought up their own way of differentiating the two grades: the established eighth graders were just eighth graders, while the new eighth graders, who really should have been preparatory . . . Sirma had told her one day some time at the end of the fall. You know what the older kids call us? Fakes. Why fakes, Maya didn't get it. Because those guys are the real eighth-graders, while we're pretending to be eighth-graders, we're trying to fake them out, get it, when in fact we're nothing but a prep class—fakes. I'm not trying to fake anybody out, Maya said, and I don't get it at all, it's not like we decided what they'd call our classes. We didn't, said Sirma, but that's how it is, just go try to talk to one of the upperclassmen and when you tell him you're in eighth grade, he'll ask you: Are you an eighth or a fake? Maya didn't know any of the upperclassmen and had nothing to say to any of them, but she was indignant nonetheless. Why the hell fakes? They stayed fakes, however, right up until the class ahead of them graduated: *eighth-fakes, ninth-fakes, tenth-fakes, eleventh-fakes*, and only then did they suddenly become the one and only twelfth grade, liberated from that shameful suffix, a change which surely could have offered some kind of gratification, if they had cared in the least. Back then, however, on the first day of the new world, Maya stopped, groaned and almost burst out crying, not because it was so fatal that she had missed out on talking to some girl from her own class instead of the neighboring one, but because she really, and I mean really, had known that something would get screwed up, and look, that's exactly what happened. She pulled away from the line and set out against the human stream to get to the previous room. She took a deep breath and felt relief when she saw that the students there looked just as random and nondescript as the others, empty blackboards for acquaintance, just waiting for friendships, bad blood, crushes, and inanity to be written on them. Since was the last to come in, all the seats were taken, except one—in the back row, next to a tall and gangly boy with black hair and a dorky prepubescent moustache on his upper lip. Maya hesitated, because she preferred not to sit next to a boy, but she didn't have a choice and everyone, including the teacher, was starting to look at her. She went all the way to the other end of the room, smiled and sat down. With a breaking voice like the buzzing of a fly hitting glass, the boy introduced himself: Spartacus.

On the road, Spartacus was digging around in his backpack for water, his backpack had stayed in the back seat, Krustev couldn't fit them all in the trunk, and Spartacus had to untie his mat and loosen the straps to get the bottle out, while Sirma made fun of him for not putting his water in a side pocket. From that first day when Maya had met Spartacus, he was constantly digging around in all sorts of backpacks, bags, satchels, plastic bags, and pulling the most bizarre things out of them: rare CDs and even cassettes, wax figures, which he crafted himself at home, pieces of candy that looked suspiciously like pills, flying sheets of paper, which he wrote funny sayings on, used bus tickets, ketchup-stained cash. When she had sat down next to him in the back row, she was convinced he would annoy her. Lord only knows what he'd come up with to show off, to impress her, most likely he'd draw on the desk. The desk, however, had already been covered by Spartacus's predecessor (someone from the *real* eighth grade), and the boy did nothing more notable than chewing on his pen. The introductions had begun. Each person got up, turned towards the class and said a few words about himself: usually only his name, what school he was coming from and how many years he had been studying English, now and then somebody would brag that he was on the basketball team or played guitar. Maya diligently tried to remember the connections between the faces and names, but when the introductions were finally over, she discovered that most of the desks remained blank spaces and only here and there did she manage to connect the two most visible constituent parts of her new classmates. Spartacus turned to her for the first time: Do you remember anybody? No one said anything that might help me remember their name. *His or her* name, Maya corrected him and he fell silent, flustered. What's my name, she asked him. Uhh . . . Joanna? No, no I'm just kidding, I remember you for sure, you're Diana. He chuckled in satisfaction at his own joke. Very funny, Maya said.

There were two reasons to stay at the same desk with Spartacus. First, she felt awkward moving, it would have seemed rude. Second, there was nowhere for her to move to: did everyone really like their new desk-mates so much or did everyone feel the same awkwardness or perhaps they were just lazy, but no pair from the first day changed places until much later. Quite soon the others began whispering, look, the first romance in the class had already sprung up. Maya could not imagine falling in love with Spartacus, nor did he show any particular interest in her. They cautiously felt out some shared terrain: he was into soccer and rock, Maya had nothing to say about the first topic, but they more or less saw eye-to-eye where rock was concerned. Maya smiled, how had their conversations gone in those first days, maximally reduced to the catechistic formula. Have you heard so-and-so? Yeah. And have you heard so-and-so? Nope. Oh man, you gotta hear 'em. Okay. And have you heard so-and-so? They went on like that for fifteen minutes and felt immense satisfaction upon grasping even the most superficial signals marking them as kindred souls. At thirteen, Maya thought to herself, you really can become friends with someone merely because you both listen to Zeppelin. Which might sound unfair towards someone you have grown so close to, but after all, there had been some beginning when you were strangers and it had to start from somewhere. It had taken quite some time, however. For the first few months, Maya mainly hung out with a couple girls who walked home in the same direction, they got on the bus together, only to scatter at different stops, yes, that was the other automatic system for establishing initial relationships when you were a *rabbit-fake*: one became friends with the people one walked home from school with, and not the other way around.

Is it too windy back there, Elena's father asked. He had opened his window and Maya watched him thirstily drinking in the mountain air, heavy with the scent of pine sap. Spartacus and Sirma said it wasn't. They discussed the Rhodope mountain chalets. Or rather, they recalled shared stories, because, of course, they had made the rounds of the Rhodope chalets in question together, the three of them. Maya struggled to think of when exactly she had met them: strange, she remembered everything so clearly, but precisely this, such a key moment, escaped her. Had she and Spartacus gone to the snack bar and there, in front of them in line, was that girl from the neighboring class with the army-surplus bag and the ironic smile? Even though back then, in that first month, the math teacher was on extended leave and the gym teacher had agreed to combined their classes, so neither group would have big holes in their schedules, so they had had gym together, forming huge mobs on the soccer field or basketball court, and in general everything had turned into one big goof-off fest, she might have met them then, or perhaps as late as the green school in December, although that was unlikely, it had to have been earlier, because by the time of the green school the three of them were already hanging out together. On the other hand, Maya remembered very well when and how things had abruptly gotten complicated and how she, to her own most sincere astonishment, had felt helpless and biting jealousy.

She and her mother had gone out to buy her some jeans. They had already been making the rounds of the stores on the main shopping street for more than an hour in the March slush and they couldn't find anything that fit both her and her budget, as well as fulfilling Maya's light-beige color requirement. They were just coming out of yet another store and Maya was about to tell her mother that she couldn't take it anymore and was ready to acquiesce to the most pedestrian blue denim just to get it over with, when Sirma and Spartacus appeared on the sidewalk in front of her. They were absorbed in conversation, Spartacus jutted up a whole head above her and was nodding so vigorously that his poofy hair, which he was trying to grow out, bobbed rhythmically and made him look a bit like a poodle. Sirma was explaining something excitedly and looked unusually pleased with herself. Maya stared. She would've pretended not to see them, she would've let them pass and given them the third degree on Monday, but from his height Spartacus noticed her, at first he jumped, but then he started waving ecstatically. Talk about theatrics! Sirma's black curls were positively glowing. Hey, what are you doing here, Maya? I'd ask the same of you; Mom, these are my schoolmates; ohhh, it's so nice to meet you, so you're Sirma and Spartacus, I've heard a lot about you, why don't you come over some time, in a matter of seconds her mother's sharp eye had managed to look them over carefully, pausing on Sirma's scrawl-covered army-surplus bag and the pins on Spartacus's jacket, while they giggled idiotically and explained that a new music store had opened up further down the street. Maya was livid. She wished them a pleasant afternoon, went into the next store with her mom and—oh, parody of wonders!—finally discovered the yearned-for light-beige jeans, which according to her mother fit her perfectly, really, said Maya, well, Okay then.

And on Monday she headed for school in her light-beige jeans, while under her coat, unbeknownst to her mother, who would have been shocked at such recklessness, it was still winter, after all, she wore only a tight pink shirt, which had shrunk sufficiently to accentuate her breasts and show her navel, she put on lipstick, she would've put on more make-up if her mother had already left for work, but there was no way to do so now, she made herself up for the first time a whole three months later for a party and the results were catastrophic, so she went to school like that, purposely dawdling on the way so she would arrive a minute or two after the teacher, she took off her jacket and was left in her pink shirt, she burst into the classroom triumphantly and . . . Spartacus wasn't there. She sat at the desk alone. Ways for expressing repeated past action: *past continuous tense, used to, would. I used to go out often with my friends.* During the break, Sirma herself popped into their room, hugged her and informed her that the music store was great and that Spartacus was sick with the flu.

When Spartacus returned to school, however, everything seemed to continue as before, the three of them went out together and Maya didn't see any signs of a greater intimacy between Sirma and him, which annoyed her all the more, because the awful anticipation of seeing them kissing at any moment ate away at her. One afternoon, when she was home alone, she sat down in front of the mirror with a cup of coffee and started asking herself questions out loud. The goal of the interrogation was to find out what was bothering her. Did she like Spartacus? If she didn't like him, what did she have against Sirma going with him? She couldn't really expect all of their relations to develop in a triangle, in which no corner was ever left out. Well yes, she told herself, in fact, that was exactly what she expected. And to be frank, from a certain moment on things really did begin to happen that way, they did everything as a trio and Maya didn't find it strange, she had never found it strange, but that really had begun later. A whole month passed before Spartacus and Sirma announced they were a couple. Maya kept hanging out with them and they didn't seem to have anything against it. What's more: Sirma started acting warmer, trusting her with more things, her eyes seemed less and less like mocking blue beads when she talked to her. Maya admitted that Sirma was very pretty, but she also thought that she herself was nothing to be scoffed at, either. Maya got used to Sirma and Spartacus being together and no longer shuddered when they kissed, but, in fact, this happened only rarely. Besides, at that same party where she had gone slathered with foundation and with eye-shadow ringing her eyes, looking as if her father had beaten her, she drank vodka for the first time, as an experiment, since at the previous party another girl had gotten drunk on vodka and hooked up with the host's neighbor; and the experiment suggested that perhaps vodka has an automatic effect because after she got drunk at one point she suddenly found herself in the parents' bedroom with the birthday boy pawing her, which was actually quite pleasant, Maya let him dig his huge, hot tongue into her mouth and sensed a warmth creeping along her spine when he unclasped her bra with astonishing dexterity, but she had already sobered up enough not to allow him to undress her. When they reappeared in the living room, Sirma looked at her with respect, while Spartacus went out on the balcony and tried to smoke with some unfamiliar boys. Maya never figured out how that unsuccessful attempt at smoking had led them to the brink of a fistfight, but she and Sirma quickly dragged Spartacus away, who also turned out to be quite drunk, they dragged him into the bathroom, and Sirma started pouring cold water over him, while he alternately snorted, laughed, yelled and shook his fists, his whole T-shirt was soaking and Maya, still mellow from her adventure with the birthday boy, suddenly said he was very sexy all wet like that, and Sirma burst out laughing, come on, girl, isn't one a night enough for you, but Spartacus was not in good shape at all and they slipped out with him, walking on either side and holding him up, while he howled '70s songs at the top of his lungs and when he couldn't remember how the lyrics went, he would simply repeat the same verse ad nauseum; Maya and Sirma were enjoying themselves thoroughly, ecstatic when some elderly passerby looked after them and clucked his tongue indignantly. But Spartacus sobered up quite quickly, growing gloomy and shame-faced. They argued for some time over how to see one another home without anyone coming to harm, since they found themselves more or less equidistant from their respective apartments. In the end, Spartacus and Sirma walked Maya home. It turned out to be barely nine, her mother and father were watching television in the dark living room and praised her for coming home on time, horrified, she expected them to bust her for drinking, but they were too engrossed in the film, only her brother met her in the hallway and said, whoa, Maya, just take a look at yourself; scram, twerp, she replied, but she went into the bathroom and was horrified to discover a degenerate whore with smeared make-up looking back at her from the mirror. If that's how you look after a hook-up, thanks, but I'll pass.

The guy called her the next day and asked her out. There was no trace of the frenzy and freedom of the previous evening and when he tried to draw her to him and kiss her after a long walk that made her calves ache, she herself was amazed at how easily she managed to slip away, explaining that while it had been fun and she didn't regret it, she preferred to remain just friends; perhaps she would have liked him to act more disappointed, but it was fine this way, too: she had *gotten smashed*, she had *hooked up*, and she had *dumped him*, the three beats naturally followed one another, and now Sirma could tell her welcome to the club, if she dared.

Incidentally, over the summer Sirma and Spartacus's relationship melted away in the same vague way as it had begun. Maya once again spent a whole month nursing suspicions that they were no longer together, until they finally told her that they really weren't. Shortly before that, Sirma had gone to the seaside with her parents and she seemed to have met some guy there. As far as Maya could tell, Spartacus didn't seem to be suffering particularly, he was the same as ever, crafting clay monsters and constantly discovering new bands, the three of them would go out in the heat, stop in front of the knocked-out window of some cellar-cum-convenience-store, buy beer from the clerks, who were scowling yet eager for business, and sit sweltering by the monument to the Scythian Army, as if deliberately daring the sun to suck the moisture from their bodies, the beer turned to bland broth before they managed to finish it, but they would sit there on the marble edge of the enormous monument, and in the later hours, more people would arrive along with the mercifully cool evening air, amorphous, noisy groups would form and they would join them, hanging out at the monument, drinking a beer or two and talking until their evening curfew approached, that's how more and more days passed and Maya's parents grumbled that she was wasting her time instead of taking a German class, but they weren't very insistent, because she had finished the school year with straight As, and also because, as she found out later, they were already planning their divorce.

Spartacus also took off, first for the sea, after which he was supposed to go straight to his grandparents' village, apparently it was somewhere close to the Sea of Marmara, and spend two whole weeks there. The first day after he left, it was a Saturday, Maya's brand new cell phone, whose primary purpose was to allow her mother to find her at all times, remained mute. She had nothing to do, so she went to her father and asked him for a book. He scratched his head and pulled a soft, tattered little book with the strange title *The Catcher in the Rye* off his bookshelf. Maya chased her brother out to play soccer with the neighborhood kids, closed herself up in their bedroom and read the book from cover to cover in one day, already halfway through she decided that she wanted to go with Holden Caulfield, at one point she wasn't so sure anymore that he even liked girls, at the very least his disgust at the ass-wagging Sally's short skirt was highly suspicious. She decided to call Sirma the next day and tell her about Holden, except that in the morning, while she was still eating breakfast, Sirma beat her to it and merely said three o'clock at the monument, right. It turned out that Sirma had read *The Catcher in the Rye* and Maya was slightly indignant that her friend had not felt the same frantic desire to share her experience, but it turned out that Sirma had something far more substantial to share. She really had met another guy at the seaside. And not only had they met, they had slept together— Sirma said *we fucked*, and now Maya suddenly and sharply recalled the shock that word had evoked in her, not the word itself, but its place in the whole situation, Sirma's ability, her desire to impart so much aggression and contempt on the intimacy of her own body, she turned away slightly, glanced at her furtively and smiled, Sirma really was a bitch then, most of all to herself. That afternoon at the monument Maya couldn't think of anything more intelligent to ask other than *how was it* and Sirma with the same biting irony described the act as if it were a scene from a silent comedy, filled with slips, pratfalls and stumbles, and Maya, despite her disbelief, started laughing, albeit nervously, Sirma also started laughing and without that air of superiority, no less, which usually tinged her laugh, how strange that it was devoid of that superiority right then, at the moment when Maya most keenly felt how much her friend had outstripped her, she kept telling herself what a baby she was. She *lost hers* quite a bit later and now it seemed normal to her, but then, during that summer of the monument they had been only fourteen and she, with all of her feelings of inferiority, had wondered at Sirma, why was she in such a rush, especially when she found out it had all happened in one night, the guy was actually from Philippopolis and they surely wouldn't see each other again, which, Sirma said, was for the best. Maya didn't think she would sleep with a man just like that, for one night, especially not for the first time, but decided to keep quiet, instead she asked about the details, since Sirma clearly relished telling them: where had they done it, so did he have an apartment, he had rented a room, they had met on the beach, in the evening she had convinced her parents to let her go out with Eugenia, the daughter of the friends they were at the seaside with, and that's how it had happened, Eugenia was also fooling around with another dude, but she was eighteen, just like Sirma's guy had been, in fact. Maya now felt somehow jealous, but not of the nameless *stud* from Philippopolis, but of this Eugenia, who had surely given her friend advice, who had taken her and shoved her into the hands of that wanker. Sirma didn't mention anything more about her. Maya asked her whether Spartacus knew. Yeah, Sirma said, I told him before he left, so is that why you broke up, actually, no, Sirma said, anyway, what does breaking up mean, what does leaving mean, you, me, and Spartacus are much closer than we could ever be with anyone else, and a single *fuck* isn't going to change that. Maya felt a warm wave engulf her, she surely blushed, her stomach clenched, she wanted to say something fitting, but she couldn't, Sirma had articulated what she had been thinking the whole time, what she had wanted to be, and now here it was alive and real, the truth itself; just then her phone buzzed, it was a text from Spartacus, it's really lame here, the sea is choppy and you can't swim, Chris Cornell has a new band, the album's coming out this fall.

[3] They stopped again: Krustev wanted another coffee. It was a swanky place—a newly constructed white building in pseudo old-fashioned style, with decorative black half-timbering, red roof tiles, and a concrete wall with stones stuck into it, and if you went inside, it turned out that the whole back wall was glassed-in, overlooking a private breeding pool. They sat down at one of the characterless tables draped with white tablecloths. They were practically the only customers: three fat, swarthy men in warm-up suits sat at a table near the bar, silently smoking and slurping hot tripe soup, which filled the hall with the life-affirming scent of garlic and vinegar. If the ancients had created a sculptural group representing the hangover, that is most likely what it would've looked like. Although back then the men definitely wouldn't have been in warm-up suits, but naked. Spartacus puffed his cheeks out, trying not to laugh. These bodies surely wouldn't have pleased Praxiteles. Over the past few months he had gotten interested in ancient art, at first despite himself, since after he'd taken the year off he had started working at a tourist agency, they called him every week or two to lead groups or to help with the writing and translation of various brochures and info packets, that was perfect for him, unwittingly, however, the subject had hooked him and he had crossed some boundary beyond which he had begun thinking about aesthetics in ancient terms, understanding the codes and messages, and he was now capable of sincerely delighting in all those armless torsos and arrogant faces with wounded noses.

I'm not hungry, Krustev said, but it's already past noon, so eat something if you want and don't worry, it's on me. Let's get a trout a piece, Sirma said. Maya started protesting Krustev's plan to treat them, but he just shrugged. If you want trout, I'll go check out the breeding pool. They didn't get it. To see what kind of shape it's in, Krustev explained. You do know, right, that trout live in clear, running water. The breeding pool is a compromise of sorts, because, of course, it's hard to build a pub right on the banks of a rushing river where trout spawn and to catch them straight from there; however, most breeding pools are full of mud, the water is stagnant, the fish don't budge, and that, of course, affects their quality. Well, we're not that fussy, Spartacus said, but in any case, I, for one, am not hungry yet. I dunno, this place doesn't really whet my appetite. A sandwich and a thermos out on the grass, now that's something else entirely, Maya agreed. So they remained in the dark as to the living standard of the local trout and drank another round of coffee. Spartacus sensed his body's resistance to the artificially inspired liveliness. He had gotten up at six. He had eaten a roll, packed his bag and left, while his mother, as usual, had gotten up to see him off at the door with admonitions to be careful. They were meeting at Sirma's studio and while riding there on the somnolent bus, he wondered at his own stupidity—why hadn't he done like Maya, who had packed her bag the previous day, brought it over to Sirma's and slept there. The two of them had overslept, of course: he rang the doorbell at length, Sirma finally answered with a yawn and waved him in. You couldn't talk to her until she'd had her coffee. Then they had to eat breakfast. It was past eight when they left, and it took them another half-hour to get outside the city on the rickety, reeking bus and to set up their ambush. They got picked up quickly, as they always did when the three of them hitched together. The man was sleepy and noncommunicative, but he clearly felt better in their company, he was going to Philippopolis, but he circled the city and left them on the outskirts so they could more easily continue south, he smiled at them and told them to have a nice trip. They waited for the next car. It wasn't a highway, mostly locals took this road and the few cars that appeared going their direction usually turned out to be packed to bursting with cabbage, empty crates, and mysterious black sacks. Finally some ancient Scythian junker stopped for them, a true relic from the times of the Eurasian Alliance, out of which leapt a jolly middle-aged windbag who cheerfully announced: Step into the Caucasian Ford! Loaded with four people and heavy backpacks, the *Caucasian Ford* sputtered down the road, while the windbag showered them with information about his personage. He was a writer (a member of the Association of Independent Thracian Writers), he had five published books—two novels and three collections of poetry—and now was writing his third novel, to balance things out, heh heh. What are you studying, kids? Llllllaw? Frrrrrrench? What about you, my girl? Arrrrrrchitecture?! Aha, a kindred soul! art is a magnificent thing, yes indeedy, but you gotta think about earning your daily bread, buuut! as it says in the Gospel, man does not live by bread alone, no sirree, he does not live by bread alone! he needs wine, too, heh heh heh. I, for my part, am a writer. Two novels and thrrrree! collections of poetry! Where are you heading, kids? To the Aegean? Well, isn't that nice, but why'd you come this way, why not take the highway, here you better be ready to sssssslosh! around the curves, and besides, there's not much traffic, goll dang it, not much traffic at all, this region has gone to the dogs, I'm from here, from the Rhodopes, from a vvvillage, Katuntsi's the name of it, but I've long since moved to the city, but now! I'm off to see what's going on in the vvvillage! to see the old house, well now my brother's living there, the man retired with a capital R and up and went back to the vvvillage, and he was right about that, do y'all live in Sevtopolis then? Yes, Maya said patiently. Good God damn, the windbag said, but that Sevtopolis is one big mmmadhouse. The vvvvillage is nice, you can write there. Maybe there! is where I'll go this summer to finish my novel. Spartacus politely inquired as to what the novel was about. I write about people, I do, the windbag warmed up, about ordinary folks with a capital F! But I think up some plots for 'em! All kinds of stories, this 'n that, all intricate-like, so there's a thrrrill to it!—and just guess how I've twisted around this story with a capital S now! it's a love story with a capital L, buuut! at one point the woman accidentally stumbles across her husband's test results—HIVeeee! positive. And she just loses it, right, 'cause she is preggers with a capital P! And that's just the first twist of many . . . Buuut! I won't give away the ending so y'all will buy the book when it comes out! They promised to do so. Fortunately, the turn-off for Katuntsi came up quickly and the windbag left them by the exit. Well now, he said, what'd I tell ya? that Caucasian Ford did the job with a capital J, as did I right along with it! Well, happy trails! Buuut! tell your friends that a real live writer with a capital W drove you! If you ask me, Spartacus said as the Caucasian Ford puttered away down the dirt road towards Katuntsi, before becoming a writer, that guy was army with a capital A. The girls giggled. That was entertaining, said Sirma, buuut! we're gonna be stuck here on this bumblefuck road for a good long time. However, they hadn't been waiting more than two minutes when a shiny red car appeared on the road, they immediately stuck out their thumbs and the car stopped. A middle-aged man poked his head out the window and Sirma yelled: Where are you going? I don't know, the man said. It doesn't matter to me. Get in.

The mountains seemed to relax a bit, the road came out of the ravines, feeling freer and stretching its shoulders. The first border of the new Thracian state right after the Liberation ran through here somewhere, damn, what a lot of work, Spartacus said to himself, and plenty of dead soldiers until we managed to claw our way to the White Sea, a White Sea outlet at any price, that's what it said in *The Outline*, the document signed by the leaders of the Thracian revolution, Thrace on three seas: the Black and White Seas plus the Sea of Marmara; he wasn't proud of the military exploits, he was more ashamed of the bones scattered over the whole peninsula, while *The Outline* itself sounded a little like a geography textbook which listed the territories that had to be included in the future Thracian state, once they were freed from the Macedonian yoke, and besides the Aegean Region, special attention had been given to the Ludogorie Region, primordial Thracian territory, that's what it said in *The Outline*, Spartacus shook his head, how well he remembered that text, back in school they had been forced to learn it by heart. In some other time, in some other history, perhaps things would have been different, but during the Liberation the European powers left the Ludogorie within the borders of Dacia and for the first half-century or so of its existence, the new Thracian state had waged three wars against the Dacians and one allied with them against Phrygia, not counting the wars against the remnants of Macedonia, as a result of which the unifier-king—with the help of Hitler, of course—had managed to unite with the Ludogorie as well, before the communists did him in and filled the Ludogorie with oil-producing roses; but after that, during their reign, the fertile brotherly Dacian people had settled in thickly alongside the oil-producing roses and began insisting that the region should once again reunite with Greater Dacia, or else break off into a second, independent Dacian state (the preferred variant, since in that case nearly a quarter of them would become ministers, diplomats, bankers and civil servants with a tendency to run to fat). When the communists attacked in '72, things with the Dacians grew complicated and in the end a quick ethnic cleansing was necessary. Spartacus's mouth twisted. Back in '72, people would say, that was a long time ago, the Dacians started rebelling and got what they deserved, now, at least, they've quieted down. Maybe it really was a long time ago. Fifteen years before I was born, Spartacus thought to himself. Those were strange times.

But perhaps every time was strange—wasn't it strange that he was now riding with Elena's father, the Beautiful Elena, she was surely the only person who had seriously threatened the unity of their trinity. Maya had brought her to them. She had introduced her ecstatically as her best friend from grade school. Damn, said Sirma. Elena was pretty, artistic and a half-Slav. Her father had once been the guitarist in Euphoria, and now he was really rich. They had learned all that gradually, however. Sirma didn't like her right from the start, or perhaps she sensed that her presence would create problems. They had long since stopped hanging out at the monument to the Scythian Army, the gathering place had shifted to the Terres Garden and Elena showed up there regularly. She brought all kinds of strange people with her: guys with dreadlocks, Slavic girls with blonde braids, they played folk instruments, *gadulkas* and *kavals*, while the rastas thumped on their djembes and blew into their didgeridoos. The first time he saw a didgeridoo, Spartacus didn't realize it was a musical instrument. The long, twisted wooden tube looked more like something the Titans would have used to play cricket. But Elena's friends had somehow figured out how to extract a bass-heavy, monotonous, hypnotizing sound from it, which spread like fog at the foot of the trees. Spartacus had tried one once out of curiosity—he couldn't get a peep out of it. They explained that you make the sound by vibrating your lips quickly. That seemed exhausting and he gave up. Then at some point the rasta guys and the Slavic girls gathered up their instruments and quit coming, but Elena stayed. Maya often showed up with her at their meetings, their trio seemed to be tending towards a quartet. Spartacus and Sirma argued several times. You can't ask Maya not to have any other friends, Spartacus would say. I'm not asking anything of the kind. Don't you have any other friends? Don't I? It's just that us three, what the three of us are, is different. I don't bring my other friends along when I'm with you. But come to think of it, why not, Spartacus objected, if your idea is for us to share everything, then we should share our friends, too. I'm gonna share one thing with you, Mr. Friendly, Sirma would say, you're into that little Slavic kitten, when she starts yowling and making eyes at you, it's like you're not even there anymore. Are you already screwing her? Listen, Spartacus would say, do I stick my nose into who you're screwing or not? We made a deal about that waaay back when, I really hope you remember. Then Sirma would shut up and back off. Her nameless Philippopolis fling from the seaside was the original sin in their alliance, the step that had made their threesome possible, it was only then that they had realized what threads they had woven between them and how they could continue on from there. Except that—Spartacus now thought in the car (and funny that he hadn't given it any thought earlier)—that original sin had stayed between him and Sirma, what did it have to do with Maya, viewed objectively, she simply did not share that tie, her foundation was missing the first thread. Perhaps that explained her sudden ecstasy over Elena. Where had she found her anyway? Some German lessons? Nice fucking place to meet, Sirma would snort. Hey, you go to drawing lessons, Spartacus would counter. Just imagine meeting your best friend from grade school there.

Oh, and I'd just pinch her cheeks with joy! Sirma would say. Of course, he hooked up with Elena and then not only Sirma, but the two of them simultaneously went crazy with jealousy. He, in all sincerity, didn't understand it: until then they had never gotten jealous over those sorts of things and at the end of the day, wasn't it at Elena's last party, in the house of the person who was now driving them to the sea, that Maya had thrown herself at that blond Slavic guy and for a whole week they had supposedly been going together, even though she surely had not told him exactly how things stood in their trio. I'm not jealous of your hook-ups, I'm not even jealous of your boyfriends, Spartacus would fume, but Sirma would reply, what, is this a signed and sealed contract? You're the one, Spartacus would strike back, who wants to make it like a contract and if you keep this up, you'll ruin everything. No, you're the one who'll ruin it, you've already ruined it, she would growl, while Maya stood aside, glowering, her arms folded across her chest. He should have trusted their female intuition even back then. They seemed to have realized that, between him and Elena, things would get serious before he himself had even realized it.

Maya and Krustev discussed the advantages and drawbacks of the resorts on the three seas, which the authors of *The Outline* had dreamed about during the nineteenth century. Krustev preferred the White Sea, thanks to its Mediterranean ambience, while Maya preferred the Black Sea, because it still had wild and untouched beaches. Spartacus had grown up with the Sea of Marmara, his grandma and grandpa's village was there, and when he was little they had always gone somewhere around there, by the way, Krustev said, now everything is totally different from when I was your age, I'm not sure if it's for better or worse. Sirma spewed out a caustic diatribe against runaway construction. They've destroyed a lot of places, Krustev agreed, on the other hand, you've got to keep in mind how much richer the country has grown thanks to tourism. Spartacus at least kept it well in mind—at the moment wasn't it his job to drag fat American retirees and ruddy German grannies around to Thracian sanctuaries, Hellenic acropolises and Roman baths? The retirees and grannies looked, clucked with forced enthusiasm, and asked when they would eat, while at the same time their children and grandchildren drank themselves blind on the astoundingly cheap alcohol in the big concrete resort complexes. Spartacus, along with half of the country, earned a not-half-bad salary from these people's boredom. But unlike half of the country, Spartacus could not fathom the fun in being dumped with a load of tourists in some poison-green hotel, frying on the beach and buying trashy souvenirs by the bagful. It's the same all over the world, Krustev shrugged. Mass tourism . . . They've got to have everything organized for them, right? Sirma said. Even their free time is regimented, hup-two-three-four! Breakfast at nine, one hour on your stomach, one hour on your back, an hour of swimming, lunch at noon, a two-hour nap, an hour of TV, cultural attractions at five, dinner at seven, a bottle of brandy at nine, a cheap Thracian whore precisely at midnight. Krustev snorted. At the end of the day, Maya said, you keep them under control that way. The question is, however, said Krustev, who is doing the controlling? Society, Maya said. That society looks a little hazy to me, Krustev said. We all know that our personal life is under threat, that they manipulate us, that they make us clones. But who are they, the ones doing it? Just show them to me and their game is up. But how can you fight an enemy who is invisible? Well, you don't fight, Sirma says. That's precisely the trick: you refuse to play their stupid game. I'm out, man, I'm just out and I don't give a shit.

Which, in fact, is hardly the best choice, Krustev noted. But it's the only possible one, Sirma said. I can't change the world, Spartacus agreed, but I can change myself. And when you've changed yourself enough, Krustev asked, but everybody else stays the same, what do you do then? There are exceptions, Spartacus said. Here are two exceptions and that's enough for me. He hugged Sirma and pinched Maya lightly on the neck. And with that he managed to put an end to the subject. Krustev's question was worth pondering, however: he asked himself the same thing quite frequently.

The man was strange. According to what he had told them, he had simply felt like hitting the road, so he checked his credit cards, threw some luggage into the car, and took off. He had no concrete goal, he had just driven wherever he felt like, and that's how he had ended up on that road in the Rhodopes. After the *Caucasian Ford* he was definitely a good catch. Spartacus had fallen asleep almost immediately, and when he woke up Maya had suddenly blurted out to him that Elena's dad was driving them. He was drowsy and didn't catch on at first. Maya had turned around in her seat and was looking at him insistently. Nodding at him knowingly. Elena's dad. Now that was slightly dubious luck. And so as not to talk about Elena, Spartacus had started jabbering on about the driver's former band (whose first album really was very good, but afterwards they sold out) and that kept the conversation farther from his daughter. But his curiosity was immediately piqued: a forty-year-old man with a solid business who suddenly up and jumps in his car and takes off for who knows where? Perhaps he was running from something, he imagined how police cars with wailing sirens would suddenly catch up with them and a crazy chase would be on through the mountain roads, and in the end they would all plunge into a river, their bodies mangled before finally drowning. Krustev had said that he would drive them to the port in Datum, and when Sirma had suddenly invited him to continue on with them on the ferryboat, he and Maya had both turned around and looked at her, good thing Maya had managed to get a hold of herself quickly and cover it up by saying that she had just been thinking the same thing. Krustev had suggested that they might be bored with him, Spartacus had immediately denied it, not only out of politeness, he would gladly chat with him about '80s music, but in his mind he had said to himself: now we've really put our foot in it. The lesser problem was that the whole idea of hitching fell by the wayside, it was as if they had their own car with a personal chauffeur. But now a fifth person was traveling with them as well: Elena.

It had happened the classic way: the two of them had gone to get beer, the usual route from the grassy lawn to the convenience store and back, and somewhere along the way, in the flower-scented darkness, Elena had simply collapsed into his arms, he had reacted instinctively, then pulled himself together a bit and carefully set the bag of empty bottles on the path. Elena pulled him towards a nearby tree, leaned against it and kept kissing him with—that's how it had seemed to him then and he even remembered it now—slightly exaggerated passion. Her mouth had a very slight taste of beer and menthol cigarettes. The night itself controlled his hands, they were no longer his. Nocturnal fingers along her spine; a cold shiver. Was it then that she had said it was high time, and he couldn't figure out what she meant, or had it happened on the way back, because after they bought beer they stopped again to make out on a bench along the way, he didn't know how much time had passed since they had left, because his hands were the hands of the night, and the whole park was giving off its scents, brought to a boil during the day by the sweltering sun, he didn't know how much time had passed, but when they got back to the meadow Sirma and Maya were gone. Hey, how could they, Spartacus said, when you think about it, Elena said, we did take a pretty long time, and actually I think it's better this way. And they made love in the meadow, then they left the beers there, just as they were in the bag, and he took her home and they made love again, quietly, in his room, they slept only two or three hours and in the morning they silently snuck out, hungry, sleepy, and intoxicated by the mingled sweat of their bodies, they ate donuts at the taxi stand, then she caught one and headed off towards her big house outside the city. In principle she had a key to the office of one of her father's companies, a small office for a small firm, not involved in his big deals, so she could sleep there when she was out late in the city. Her parents didn't ask many questions. Spartacus couldn't help but admire them. He shook his head and stared at the crown of Boril Krustev's head. He had not yet started balding. Now that was awkward, precisely this person driving them, that is, it was awkward for Maya and Sirma, while for him it was more likely painful, at times he had the feeling that some rope of thorns tied him to the man sitting in front of him, who drove so quickly and confidently and spoke little, but Spartacus had started getting a sense of him, as if he were clinging to the three of them. Maybe back then, two years ago, Elena, too, had tried to cling to them, perhaps that night when they had gone to get beer (come on, let's go get beer, she would say after that, sly little flames lighting up her eyes), she had slept with him twice so as to weasel her way into their group, into their inviolable trio, and then she had gone with him, so as to go with *them*. No one else had showed that much ambition and it hadn't even crossed Sparta-cus's mind that it was theoretically possible for their triangle to become a square. You're sick, Elena had told him, haven't you ever had a normal relationship? The last hills of the Rhodopes were now spilling over into the green Aegean fields. They passed a car with Macedonian plates. Soon thereafter they came out onto the main road to Datum. Maya was telling Krustev something about her elementary school, Spartacus started listening, of course, it was something about Elena, it was only logical . . . And then she moved, Maya concluded. Yes, Krustev confirmed, we bought the house then and sent her to a closer school. Otherwise I would've had to drive her and pick her up every day, he added apologetically. Spartacus tried to imagine Elena in third grade. He couldn't. But maybe, it suddenly occurred to him, maybe there isn't just one Elena, there are lots of Elenas and every one of the four of us here in the car knows one of them. He looked out through the window, but the fields outside had nothing interesting to offer. Hey, Sirma said, penny for your thoughts?

[4] It was stupid, but lately all older men somehow reminded her of her professor of façade architecture. Her professor had called her in to his office hours, I'm impressed by your work, Sirma. She was dressed in jeans and a sporty jacket, and she had made an effort to smell like cigarettes, because the professor looked like the type to rent an apartment across from a kindergarten. But he turned out to have entirely something different in mind. He offered her a job at his design agency, if you accept, he said, I believe I can teach you much more than your classmates will learn. Sirma had felt like giving him a good hard slap. All the professors here were like that: they spewed out inanities for two hours at their lectures,

making very sure not to teach their students anything so as not to create competition for themselves. And they looked like people who rented apartments across from kindergartens. Sometimes she felt like blowing them all away.

Although Krustev actually looked quite a bit younger. So he must've become a father at their age. His life had surely passed at high speed. And now somebody had jammed a stick in the spokes: Crrrack! And he'd taken off alone in his car. And how Maya and Spartacus had jumped when she had invited him to come with them. She had done it on impulse, maybe just to see their faces. Since Maya had foisted Elena on them back then and had caused such a crisis, why shouldn't she now be stuck with Elena's father tagging along with them, driving them, what's more, the man obviously was in need of company, even though he may not have realized that himself, interesting, Sirma wondered, are they all such nutjobs, the whole family, for the moment, at least, Krustev seemed far more likeable than his daughter, although when you stopped to think about it, it was precisely Elena's craziness that had changed some things completely and in the end had brought them even closer, it was then, right, after she had finally cleared off, that they had held the first *mysteries*. Spartacus and Maya hadn't wanted to, she had insisted. If things don't evolve now, we're lost, that's what she had told them, now here's evolution for you, I suggest once a month, and I don't care who you play around with the rest of the time. It had been working well. There were only a few days left until the next mysteries.

Besides, Sirma was convinced that the way she and Maya had reacted back then, which had been more or less the same, suggested that things had already passed the point of no return and that sooner or later they would end up there. They were no longer kids, they were eighteen and they could approach things a little more thoughtfully, to a certain extent that was why Sirma was so furious with Spartacus, things were obvious and all he had to do was slightly redirect the energy from his little head to his big one, but, of course, the sudden, screaming burst of jealousy was something else entirely, something totally unexpected, Sirma was amazed at herself. Surely, she thought to herself later, that was nothing new for Maya, she was definitely jealous of them during their first year as fakes, before everything really started, but that was kid stuff, of course, yet Maya still had some experience with jealousy, and it was as if she was a step ahead of Sirma in terms of experience for the first time. But Elena herself had mucked things up. If she hadn't rushed to sleep with Spartacus, Sirma told herself, staring at her father's hands on the wheel, if instead she had staked her bet on Maya, on *her best friend from grade school*, not in the sense of sleeping with her, ha ha, but just leaving Maya to push her into the middle of their triangle, as she had done in the beginning, perhaps it would have been much harder to deal with her. Maya was very stubborn. Something had to whack her hard upside the head to change her mind, and then she would turn 180 degrees. She's so nice, she's so cool, she's got great friends, okay, obviously she can't be a part of *us*, there's just no way that could happen, there's really no way, Sirma added, it'd be like wanting her to grow a cock, Spartacus shrugged, that was before that night when they'd gone for beer, and she had been so furious then, on the one hand she had long since realized where things were head-ing, but how he had left them sitting there on the grass waiting for their stupid beer, that just took the cake. He, of course, called her the next morning, and after she hung up, Sirma caught herself wondering if he had called her or Maya first. And good thing she caught herself, because that would have been the result of Elena's scheming, trying to make them all fight over Spartacus, otherwise, whatever the two of them thought, Sirma in principle had nothing against other people hanging around them, Elena seemed fun and good-natured, but she simply had to know where her rights ended, well, she didn't know, and besides Sirma had felt some kind of instinctive animosity towards her as soon as she had seen her, she couldn't figure out why for a long time. What about her father? It was only now that she seriously asked herself why she had invited him to come with them and discovered that she didn't know. Just like that, a momentary impulse, perhaps just the same as when he had jumped in his car early that morning, but he had done it because he had issues, so did that mean that she or maybe they had issues with themselves? The man's hands didn't flinch on the wheel and that was strange, because otherwise they looked mercurial in some way, which Maya surely would have said was cute, but which Sirma found exhausting. She tried to imagine her own father picking up three hitchhikers, but her father rarely traveled, before he couldn't stay in one place, now he just sat in his office, diffusing the depressed pride of an ex-politician. While this guy was an ex-musician and didn't actually seem like anybody's father at all, maybe Elena had popped up just like that in the world, having conceived herself in her mother's belly and brashly cleared a trail to the outside with her tiny yet tough little hands, Elena didn't fit with the idea of a family; while Sirma would have to call her own family at some point to tell them she was on Thasos and that the studio was empty, they would simply say fine, stop by for tea when you get back, always tea, god damn it, and never coffee. Her father answered fine to everything, could that be why he had gotten into politics or why he had left politics so ignobly, but he had answered fine to everything ever since she was little, she could remember how they had gone to the seaside for the first time, that was one of her first clear memories, they had gone to the beach and her parents had stripped down to their bathing suits and told the kids to strip down, too, but they didn't put any bathing suits on them and Sirma had seen the funny little potato sprouting between her brother's legs, now she wondered if she could really have noticed it for the first time at age three, but in any case that's how she remembered it, she had turned to her parents and said he's got something growing between his legs, her mother had started giggling, while her father had simply said fine and kept slathering himself with sunscreen, so why don't I have one of those, she had asked, because you're a girl, her brother had announced triumphantly and asked whether he could go build a sandcastle by the water, fine, her father had said, but take Sirma with you, fine.

Elena's father suddenly asked, so where will you stay on Thasos. We'll camp, Spartacus replied immediately, patting the tent tied to his backpack which a short while earlier had prevented him from taking out his water bottle, Krustev fell awkwardly silent. Maybe this was their chance to ditch him, she hesitated for a moment; and again Sirma, this time not impulsively but completely consciously, because she believed that when things reached a certain point you had to see them through or at least patiently leave them alone to see themselves through to the end, so she completely consciously added, you're coming, right? Well, yeah, Krustev said. Except in that case I'll need to buy a tent. When we get to Datum I can take care of that, too. He probably smiled, but Sirma couldn't see him from the backseat, she only saw his fingers happily drumming out a few bars on the steering wheel. Now that's man-talk for you, she said. I didn't know there were campgrounds on Thasos, Krustev said, there are, Sirma confirmed, they left one next the woods and it's really cool, let's just hope it's not full. Krustev asked if it had running water and electricity, it has both running water and electricity, Sirma told him, Krustev said fine. And she smiled, but Krustev's *fine* sounded peppy in comparison to her father's tired and apathetic *fine*, she had gradually gotten so tired of her parents' tiredness that she had had to drink four cups of coffee a day and in a moment of enlightenment had realized that it was time to move out. Her father had again said fine, do you want the attic apartment, her mother had asked, yes, said Sirma, I can set up a studio there, in fact, the attic had been set up as a studio right when they bought it, light and sufficiently roomy, good thing we thought to buy before prices jumped, her father had said, it's a nightmare now, thanks to those crooks . . . Her brother was studying in Holland and the attic awaited her alone. The contract with the renter required them to give a month's notice, Sirma felt a bit bad about this, she'd seen the guy, she'd gone to pick up the rent a few times and he was actually quite nice, she couldn't deny that various things had crossed her mind, but in any case now she needed to move out and live on her own, ever since her brother had left it had become completely intolerable, not that with him things had been much better, but at least there had been some pulse, now it was a complete dead zone, her father tried to stay at the office as late as he could, her mother came home from work and immediately put on CDs of classical music, Sirma had nothing against chatting with her, but she was always trying to win her over to Haydn or Couperin, sorry, Mom, Sirma would say, but this music doesn't speak to me at all, her mother would pout, pull X-rays of teeth out of her bag and start studying them with feigned interest. So they called the renter, he obediently found another apartment, then superficial yet rather prolonged renovations began, with every passing day the studio looked brighter and Sirma would constantly give Maya and Spartacus updates about how the renovations were coming along, perfect, we can hold the mysteries there, Spartacus suggested and Sirma was taken aback because she hadn't thought about that, but yes, it was completely logical. The renovations ended, she moved in and threw a party that nullified a good part of what had been done, she had invited tons of people, including almost her whole high school class, the ones who were still in Thrace, of course, and almost all of them came, even Petsi, poor old Petsi, he had fallen in love with her sophomore year, back then he had been a puny little guy with long arms and a cracking voice whose favorite topic of conversation was shaving. Sirma never figured out how she had suddenly become the object of his affections, as if Petsi had been sitting there for a long time, observing his female classmates and after many months of reflection had decided to fall in love with her. She realized this thanks to his persistent attempts to chat her up at recess, while she hurried to meet up with Spartacus and Maya, and thanks to the complicated seating shifts that began occurring in the classroom because Petsi was constantly trying to maneuver such that he would be sitting behind her. She found it really funny, but also felt sorry for him, the kid was a bit of a dork, the others looked down on him and maybe he had decided to bowl them over all at once by seducing her, Sirma wasn't born yesterday and knew very well that the guys in her class were checking her out, she wondered if they thought about her when they masturbated in the shower, maybe that's what had been going through Petsi's head in the beginning, but he was acting so ridiculous that maybe he really had fallen in love. Sirma tried to act like she didn't notice him. She complained to Maya and Spartacus, they knew him in passing, Spartacus, who at that time was getting busy with some girl from the German high school and who seemed to imagine that Sirma and Maya would be jealous on that account, warned her that Petsi struck him as a hardcore dreamer and surely would not give up so easily. Sirma didn't notice anything changing. But one morning, shortly after she had gotten up, her phone rang, it was Petsi, who had never called her on the phone before, and he barked out "Happy holidays!" Sirma was confused for a second, what holiday, he doesn't think it's my birthday, does he, but then she remembered that it was March 8—International Women's Day—and almost burst out laughing, but instead said thank you, Petsi, and he went on: I need to ask you a very serious question. Go ahead, Petsi, she mumbled, assuming that now he would ask her out, but on the other end of the line he busted out directly with: *Do you like me?* Sirma was speechless, this was the strangest line anyone had ever used on her, in fact, perhaps little old Petsi, for some unknown reason, had enormous self-confidence, and instead of talking about his own feelings, which would have again been a pathetic move, he preferred first to inquire about hers. Uh, well, Petsi, she said, actually, no, I don't like you that way. I knew you liked me . . . Yeah, that's what I figured, Petsi said coldly. You know how it is, she was getting more and more flustered. I mean, either it happens or it doesn't, I'm sorry, but I don't like you that way, but we can still be friends, right? They agreed to stay friends, even though they weren't actually friends in the first place to be able to remain so, nor would they become friends later, Sirma hung up, she happened to be right in front of the big mirror in the entryway and saw that she had an exceptionally stupid grin on her face. Because Petsi has infected me with his stupidity, she suddenly steamed and considered putting him in his place by telling the whole story to the class gossips, but she quickly thought better of it; in the end the poor kid surely had no experience with women whatsoever and was just doing what he could. But on the very next day she realized with astonishment that other guys she knew took March 8 as a particularly fitting occasion for declaring their love. Snickering, Spartacus told them how a kid in another class, nicknamed Smirk, liked some chick from the new eighth grade, Spartacus knew the whole story in detail, because the chick was a friend of his cousin, and one time he made the mistake of mentioning this in front of Smirk and the latter started grilling him for all kinds of information, and not just him, Spartacus said, he built up a whole spy network to gather useful information about the girl. Yesterday Spartacus had been drinking beer with their class and Smirk, with an enviable sense of humor, had told of his spectacular flop. He had stalked her in the schoolyard and gone over to give her a rose, because, Spartacus sniggered, his grandpa had won over his grandma that way back in the day. Sirma and Maya burst out laughing, no way, he didn't really say that? Yeah, he did, Spartacus replied, the man told it just like that and laughed a lot himself, too, what can you do—he's Smirk, right?! So anyway, he goes over with a rose like his gramps, although surely his grandpa had cornered his grandma alone, but our man Smirk took the twins along for moral support . . . The twins were metalheads from the class in question, absolutely identical, on the short side, with long hair and leather jackets, the only way to tell them apart was by their T-shirts: one wore an Iron Maiden T-shirt, and the other a Manowar shirt so they called him the *Manowarrior*, while the other was simply *the twin*. For some reason, the short twins always roamed the hallways with a taller classmate between them and Sirma had long since noted that this configuration looked like a cock. So he goes over with the twins, right, Spartacus continued, 'cause she's leaning on the railing with a friend of hers, he hands her the rose and asks her what her name is. Sirma let out a squeal. He had interrogated me, right, Spartacus said, and I had told him that the girl lives in West Park, so now he asks her where she lives and she mumbles West Park and now—Spartacus lifted a finger triumphantly—this is where the twins come in, because Smirk turns to them and roars in frenzied ecstasy: Whooooooa, man, they live in West Park, too!!! And that was supposed to serve as a topic to melt the ice definitively, however, the girl muttered in alarm thanks a lot for the rose but I already have a boyfriend, now she doesn't have a boyfriend, of course, Spartacus said, and Smirk knows that, he's done his homework, but he gets the message, he's a reasonable guy, after all. But he did say that he's not gonna work with his grandpa's know-how from now on. And at the party Sirma threw to inaugurate the studio, Petsi showed up with a girlfriend and Sirma was suddenly really happy for him, she talked to the girl for a long time, she was a good catch, Petsi had obviously learned the ropes, sometimes things don't work for you with one group of people, you feel smothered, and when you escape them, you suddenly blossom, she thought to herself.

Lucky we managed to hang on to these two islands, Maya chimed in from the front seat, we could've ended up with no islands at all. Lots of luck, Spartacus said, adding: And *a li'l thrashing*, imitating the thick Illyrian dialect of a certain prime minister who had made his mark on history with that phrase alone, which illustrated his style of government: *With kindness, with gentleness, and with a li'l thrashing*. Elena's father again said how easy it was to travel now, they didn't need visas, and they could hop from island to island. *Island-hopping*, Spartacus put in, the Swedish retirees show up and start hopping from island to island, we could hop to some other island afterwards, too, Krustev suggested, let's go to Rhodes, Sirma said, to check out my roots at the source, oh what, so you're from Rhodes now? Spartacus was confused, from somewhere there, Sirma replied, didn't I tell you, from Lydia, some great-grandfather of mine came from there, he could've been from Rhodes, they say it's a nice place and that knights stroll around the streets, she finished with a yawn. That's a pretty serious hop, from Thasos to Rhodes, said Maya. *Hic Rhodus, hic salta*, Spartacus declared, Sirma looked at him in confusion, what? Nothing, said Spartacus, it's a Latin saying. There might be some ferryboats, Krustev suggested, again drumming his fingers on the wheel, there must be a way to reach Rhodes from Thasos by sea, you've got time, right? We've got time, Sirma said, but money is a slightly different story, don't worry about money, Krustev said, come on now, Maya cut in, you offered us a ride, not an allowance, Krustev shrugged and said that he was having a good time with them, that he had enough money, not that he meant anything by it, just so they knew if need be. Don't you have a yacht, Sirma asked, now that would've been a catch, to hitch a ride not only from a car but from a yacht to boot, *they sold off the factories and bought themselves yaaachts*, her father would say in disgust when talking about his former fellow party members, well, if only you'd bought yourself one, too, she would reply, whereupon he would explode briefly, then suddenly fall silent, muttering fine. Actually, I don't have a yacht, Elena's father said, and I can't even swim, we Slavs are rather suspicious of any surface that can't be plowed and planted, I was kidding, Sirma said, as was I, he said, but it's the truth, we're landlubbers. You really can't swim, Spartacus wondered, I mean, swimming is the whole point of going to the beach, otherwise what are you gonna do there, just fry in the sun or play cards? And yell at your kids, Krustev added, I'm sure it would be more fun if I could swim, but in any case I never learned, but back in the day going to the seaside and sitting on the beach for at least half a day, that was our idea of a vacation, I'm talking about when I was five or six, that was something new for my parents, I don't know if they really even liked it or just went along with the trend, we'd rent an apartment on the seaside and go to the beach with our own umbrellas so we wouldn't have to pay for them, that was an option back then, all this hysteria about hotels and private beaches hadn't yet begun or was just beginning, I had fun, all kids surely have fun at the beach, and later, of course, whole crowds of us would go, huge groups with tents, guitars, girls and some more dubious things as well; we took Elena to the seaside ever since she was born, that's how much sense we had, but be that as it may, I've got a fair amount of experience with camping, never mind that it was a while ago, true, back then we didn't insist on having electricity and running water, at least not before Elena was born, so he'd seen her in the mirror, Sirma thought, he had seen her smirk when he asked whether there was electricity and running water at the campground and she felt a little ashamed, maybe this person had actually had a much wilder youth than they had. He had gotten so carried away with his monologue that he was waving his right hand in the air. Okay, we'll teach you to swim then, she said. Krustev started laughing, it's too late for me to learn anything whatsoever, don't give me that, Sirma said, if you want, we can make a deal, we'll teach you to swim, and you think up something to teach us. We really got lucky with him, she thought, and he really got lucky with us, but let's just see what will come out of this whole lucky story. Rhodes, she whispered to herself, a name that digs into the mouth like a drill, it sounds brutally seductive and Krustev seemed serious, but there was that awkward moment again: since she had gone to college, she had often found herself talking to older men and even when one of them would pick up the tab for the whole table's coffee, she still felt that same hesitation, now with Elena's father it was much sharper, this person had money, he had a car, he had time and clearly needed their company, he could drive them wherever they wanted, on top of everything that was exactly what he wanted, but still, how much could they take advantage of all that, not for his sake, but for their own sake, how much would they let him spoil them, she was sure that Spartacus and Maya were thinking the same thing at that moment, but on the other hand, when else would they have the chance to go to Rhodes, plus she could call her dad and ask him about that great-grandfather, besides travelling with the guitarist from Euphoria was not bad at all. They were already entering Datum. The car in front of them was driving slowly, uncertainly, and Krustev, suddenly impatient, laid on the horn, Sirma again stared at his hands and suddenly realized why her gaze had been returning to them the whole time, she had subconsciously grasped the little detail, the tragic aberration, she remembered very clearly how when her grandfather had died, almost the first thing her grandmother had done was to move her wedding ring from her right to her left hand with a sigh, Sirma took a deep breath, as if drinking in her grandmother's sigh: like her, the widow, Boril Krustev was wearing his wedding ring on his left ring finger.

[5]

The young people insisted on splitting the bill and he gave in, once he realized that they took his insistence on treating them as aggression. He had been to that little restaurant at the port before and liked it, as a whole he liked Aegean cuisine, with its Mediterranean tang, on the surface, they looked like the same dishes as from the interior of the country, but now look, a pinch of cumin and a little fennel turned them into something completely different, and besides, the little restaurant had held out against the surge of mass tourist-fare, which meant stuffing everything you can get your hands on in the fridge into the microwave all at once, Rhodopaise surprise served jack-ass style, chicken julienne in a clay pot with soy sauce, blue cheese, and peas.

After lunch, they divided into two combat units, Sirma and Spartacus went to find out about the ferryboats, Krustev and Maya looked for an outdoor store to buy a tent, but how can you just go and buy a tent, as if it were a pound of cucumbers, confused they went to a tourist office and asked: there, of course, they had no idea where such a store might be, but on their way out, Krustev caught sight of a brochure for a store called Montblanc, the brochure was in Thracian and English, and the store was on the next street over. Krustev thanked the fat woman behind the window, who indignantly raised her eyes from her crossword puzzle, and they went to Montblanc, Maya and the salesman picked out a dark-blue tent with fiberglass poles for him, whatever that meant, reliable, light and easy to pitch, that's what the kid said, can I put it on my card, yes, of course.

They regrouped at the car, the ferryboat was leaving in half an hour, they got in line immediately, luckily there weren't many cars and they managed to wedge themselves into the monster's cold, gas-fume-laden belly. The trip took a little over an hour.

They went up on deck. Amid cigarette smoke marking off the time, two young Englishwomen with reddened faces had already stripped down to their bathing suits, their bodies resembling plastic chairs, they were drinking beer and shouting. A dark-skinned man, huddled in a worn leather jacket despite the warm weather, would glance at them from time to time, quietly groaning and averting his eyes. It wasn't clear whether he was enjoying the spectacle or not. Typical specimens, Sirma said. There were no free seats, but they found an empty corner near the railing, farther from the Englishwomen, and stared into the cheery blue water, the weather was very clear, Krustev suddenly thought how strange it was that he now found himself here, on this ferryboat, with these young people, friends of his daughter, whom he hadn't known two hours ago, and now he was going with them to Thasos, with his brand-new tent with fiberglass poles. He hadn't expected things to turn out this way, but actually, when he took the car out, he wasn't expecting anything. Good thing he didn't have Rex with him any longer, otherwise he wouldn't have been able to run off just like that without taking the dog with him, a month ago he had brought Rex to his parents, who were now living in what had once been his grandfather's house by the river, but it was no longer the last house on the edge of the village, the village had for all practical purposes become a cluster of summer homes, they were worried, why, his mother had asked, do you want to be left all alone in that house, that's exactly what he wanted, he didn't know why, but after Elena had gone back to America, he was in no condition to do anything except immerse himself in total solitude, to sink into cozy self-pity, the dog would bother him, besides it would surely feel better in his parents' tranquil care, incidentally they had hinted that he himself should live with them for a while, he had carefully but firmly turned them down and they had seemed to understand.

Irina passed away in January. It had been four months now: just as long as she'd been in a coma, still alive, without knowing it. Krustev remembered his wife's body, shrunken, thin, worn-out, and misshapen, bound by unquestioning tubes to mysterious devices which allowed it to exist a bit longer on the threshold between life and death. He felt like tubes had been stuck into him, too, pouring first fear into his blood, then hope and finally a colorless, watery liquid, the very essence of futility. You do understand, don't you, the head doctor had told him some time in October, when it was already clear that there wouldn't be any quick recovery and that they could only hope for a miracle, but miracles like that do happen, don't they, in these kinds of cases, yes, but you do understand, he had told him, that if your wife recovers, it is very possible that she will not be the same person, right now it's difficult to say how disabled she might be. Irina could come out of the coma drained of her identity, without memories, without thoughts even, without taking in anything around her, a vegetating presence in a wheelchair. Yet he had nevertheless nursed hopes until the last, he had clung to his wife after all that creeping marital coldness, after they had lived almost separately for the past four years, her boyfriend, the theater director, also came to see her as often as Krustev did, but they had asked the hospital staff to stagger their visits, neither one wanted to see the other, Krustev now remembered that there had been a similar story in one of the books he had read in the early spring, only there the husband and the lover took care of their shared wife together, it wasn't like that in his case, perhaps both of them blamed each other at least a bit for what had happened. Krustev was constantly wondering about guilt, not just whether he himself was guilty, but whether guilt even existed at all as something you could touch or feel or whether at the end of the day everything was a sea of dreams and wakings, which we all will drown in some day, a sea like that one down below, he lifted his head and saw the kids looking at him rather worriedly, so he suggested they get a beer and this time he wouldn't take no for an answer, went over to the ferryboat's concession stand and came back with four cold cans.

So why, Spartacus asked, abruptly jerking him into a completely different time, did Euphoria really break up? Good question, why had they broken up really, perhaps because the singer had started acting more and more like the head, heart, and ass of the group, or because the keyboardist was against the more commercial sound of their final years, or maybe—and this seemed the likeliest answer to Krustev—because nobody felt like playing anymore. When he stopped to think about it, they had only been around thirty—thirty-something, pretty early for exhaustion, but the rock-band life had sucked them dry unexpectedly quickly, they needed to be reborn as new people, they still had the strength and opportunity to do so, and yes, well yes, they did just that. Krustev suddenly felt, or at least he thought that he felt as if not only his mind, but his very senses were beginning to run on memories, he felt the pain from the metal strings running through his fingertips, the pain that had been so persistent in his early teenage years when he was just starting to play, later, of course, his fingers had calloused over and didn't hurt anymore. Man, you're a serious rock fan, he said to the young man and was really impressed by his taste and knowledge, Spartacus shrugged his bony shoulders humbly. Only here, on the deck where the four of them were standing together, upright, only here could Krustev get a clearer idea of what his fellow travelers looked like: the boy, tall and skinny, taller than he was, with a constantly distracted expression; the blonde Maya, who had a rather ordinary face, but lively eyes and a compact, athletic figure; and finally the slightly mysterious and distant ring-leader of the group, with curly black hair and blue eyes, Krustev guessed she had lots of admirers and then immediately wondered whether that word was even still used, the truth was that at times he felt like an old man in their company, even though he had gotten used to always being young, both in his life as a musician and in that as a businessman, he was always the youngster, they didn't take him seriously at first, then suddenly they'd be shocked at how much he'd accomplished for his age, what are forty years, he could still live another forty, and he was sure that within a week he could get back into shape after those months spent in the empty house, that he could once again feel energetic and healthy, but hey, his body would never be as quick and flexible as the bodies of these people around him ever again. He could feel the beer filling his bladder insultingly quickly, impudently squeezing his prostate, he excused himself and found the grimy toilet down below by the cars, poorly lit by a yellow bulb, his stream gushed with gurgling relief, he zipped his fly and slowly started back up the stairs, climbed up on deck and stood by himself for a while before going back to the trio.

The strangest part was that he had gradually *gotten used to* it all: the visits to the hospital, the silent Irina tangled up in plastic tubes, the white sheets, the nurses, the smell of bleach in the hallways, where men and women padded around in green pajamas. Krustev had sat by his wife's bed and talked to her in his mind, that way the words weren't left hanging in the startling absence of an answer. He had talked to her about Elena, about the dog, about the house, sometimes about business, a few times he had tried to clear up how exactly, imperceptibly and secretly, like the rotting of a seemingly sound fruit, their relationship had gone cold. Her coma couldn't turn back time, he still knew that he no longer loved Irina the way they had loved each other in their wild and sunny younger years, but now, when she inhabited the space between life and death, when she was so far from him that he couldn't reach her with words or touch, he suddenly felt close to her again, or rather he felt close to her in a new way, almost as if she were a sister. Irina was now the only person who didn't want anything from him. And even though he had secretly hoped for a miracle up to the very end, sometimes he caught himself fearing that possible moment when Irina would flutter her eyelids, heavy from sleep, the long sleep of the sea, when he thought about the undertow that was sweeping her along, Krustev shuddered and suddenly imagined how, if he put his ear to his wife's body, he would hear the sea roaring inside her, as inside a shell. She really was a shell, the form of a living creature, emptied of her soft, slimy, and slithering substance, at once alluring and repellent. And he would talk to that shell, sensing how everything around him withdrew and he was left alone with her in the white silence of the hospital room, as if time had stopped. But before Christmas, Elena had come back from the States again, pale, thin, with circles under her eyes, she had burst into tears when she saw her mother and the thread was broken, the whole quiet harmony that Krustev had built up day after day fell apart. At that moment he felt hatred for his daughter, that intruder from out of nowhere, a part of both of them, who had cunningly leapt into the world and come between them. Then he told himself that he was probably going crazy, but he couldn't shake the feeling that this young woman was a stranger to him, now much more than ever, and the shell in the hospital bed could not fill up the chasm between them, on the contrary, it opened it all the wider. And after that, shortly after New Year's, which he and his daughter had spent at home, staring at the television, almost without speaking, Irina had died. As if during that whole time she had been hesitating and had finally made a decision. Sepsis, the head doctor said, poisoning of the blood, her liver couldn't hold out, I was also hoping until the last, I'm sorry. And he really did seem sorry, perhaps he, too, had gotten used to the empty body and its plastic tubes, perhaps he had even clung to the possibility of her coming out of the coma so as to reaffirm his belief in the power of his work and his science, except that Irina had died and Krustev suddenly felt his whole life withdrawing, his senses, his memories, as if he were once again in the silent white room, only now there was nothing inside it, nothing at all, so much so that he couldn't even be sure whether he himself was there. Now, when he thought back on those days, he would tell himself that he had been on the edge. He didn't remember the funeral. He remembered how he had shut himself up at home and had sunk into the TV, watching sports channels from morning until night, he had taken his blanket out to the sofa in the living room, where he had also spent the nights, lulled to sleep by the figures running back and forth across the screen, Elena had hovered around him, they only spoke about everyday household things, she had made clumsy attempts at cooking and Krustev had gulped down her dishes without even noticing whether they were any good or not. And so several days passed, then she suddenly appeared at the start of some soccer game, sat down next to him and said *Barcelona's going to win*, Krustev suddenly sprang out of his apathy and looked at her amazed, she had never been interested in soccer and he could've sworn she didn't even know how many players were on a team, but now here she was talking about *corner kicks, offsides, and poor performance in the Champions League*, she was talking about things that sounded strange to him, as if coming from some world beyond, he perhaps wouldn't have even noticed that volleyball had been replaced with soccer, she mentioned the players' names, reacted more quickly than the commentator, kept track of who had gotten yellow cards, and when the game indeed ended with a win for Barcelona, Krustev said, yes, Barcelona won, moved his crackling joints, gingerly got up off the sofa, took a bottle of scotch from the bar, poured two glasses, set them abruptly on the table and said, so now tell me what's going on with you.

Their corner had livened up. Maya was lying on the floorboards as if ready to do push-ups and making some strange movements with her right leg, Spartacus and Sirma were watching her, their arms folded over their chests, while all around them people were knitting their brows and shaking their heads. Krustev also knit his brow in confusion, then he realized that she was demonstrating some yoga exercises, this asana is called tiger, Maya panted and got up, brushing the dust off her hands, is there a hamster asana, Sirma asked. Spartacus explained that Maya had gotten really into yoga and she wanted to recruit them as well, but they won't give in, Maya said, it's a lot more fun sitting in the park drinking beer, because you never so much as sip a beer, right, Sirma smirked, you know what, if you can drink a beer in that pose you were just in, then you win, I'll start going to this yoga of yours. Krustev was intrigued. Are you not supposed to eat meat, he asked, well, Maya replied, this is what our teacher says: A man can climb a mountain with a bag of rocks on his back, except it'll be a whole lot easier without it, I still eat meat, but I'm cutting back and trying to give it up, not just because of yoga, but still . . . Enough proselytizing, Sirma interrupted her. We're here. Krustev looked ahead, the island really was very close, a scowling crew member with a megaphone appeared and gave a spiel in an equally scowling tone, so they went back downstairs and got in the car, ready to drive off, well, Krustev said, we had to wait a while before getting on, but now we'll be one of the first ones off. Oh man, said Spartacus, I can't wait to pitch my tent. I'm sure you're going to have to help me with mine, Krustev smiled, because it looks so simple. Back in the day there was a whole philosophy to it and I can only pitch complicated tents. Fiberglass, he said to himself again, it sounded pleasantly cold.

The ferryboat spewed out its contents on land. They had no reason to stay in the city, so Krustev headed straight for the campgrounds, following Sirma's directions. It turned out to be very close and enormous, but practically empty. Krustev wondered to himself if it still wasn't a bit early for a tent on Thasos. The campground was situated at the edge of a vast but thin pine forest, the beach was surely a whole kilometer long and tents and RVs could be seen only here and there among the hedgerows dividing the sites. An RV, Krustev said to himself, now that's what we really need for this trip, it would've been perfect. But by the time he thought of this, it was too late. They offered them four neighboring sites for one-man tents, until now, Krustev, without even giving it a second thought, had imagined that the three of them would sleep together in one tent, one of those big ones, and was surprised at this betrayal of their constantly declared unity, but Spartacus explained the obvious fact that if they wanted to sleep together in one big tent, somebody would have to carry it. It was much easier for everyone to sleep in their own. What's more, you snore, Maya added. They set about pitching the tents, while their not particularly numerous neighbors watched them with the routine curiosity of old hands towards greenhorns, and to his satisfaction Krustev managed to pitch his tent with no more difficulty than the others, albeit more slowly. He set his mat and sleeping bag inside, which he had just bought from the store in Datum, and lay down for a bit to see how it was. The hard ground beneath him suddenly took him back in time, he had forgotten that feeling. Someone coughed outside and he came out, it was Maya, beaming and sunny, to find out whether everything was all right and Krustev felt as if they had the right to exercise certain fatherly concern towards him rather than the other way around, or else he was misinterpreting things, it's great, he said and looked at his watch, it was three, so if we settle up the payment quickly, we'll have time to hit the beach, Maya shrugged, even though here you're always on the beach in any case, and Krustev told himself he was being stupid, of course that's how it was, they weren't going to hurry off somewhere else, lugging striped bags of towels, sunscreen and other beach gear, the time when he had almost constantly lived like that really wasn't so far off in the past, but you get used to conveniences and the conventions of a life of luxury so quickly. Would he really look so different from them when they stripped down to their bathing suits, maybe not, his body really did feel a bit clumsy and stiff, but he didn't have a paunch thanks to his quick metabolism, his toenails were trimmed, everything should be fine. The campground attendant came back and they paid for four nights for starters, Krustev didn't offer to pay for them because he knew they would never let him, besides, if the trip stretched out sooner or later they would surely run out of cash and then they would have to fall back on his, he liked treating them and thought that if twenty years ago he had found himself in such a situation, he, too, would have resisted the other person's attempts to pick up his tab, yet deep down he would have been very pleased at such luck. How they had studied the finer points of the art of traveling with a barebones budget back in the day, of course, prices were a whole lot different back then, as were their requirements, yes, from a certain point on they had wanted to buy comfort and, in fact, he thought now, that made traveling as much like staying at home as possible, nothing from home was lacking. He came out of his tent in his swim trunks, feeling a bit awkward and constantly looking over his body, moles, hair; while waiting for the others to come out he wondered whether he should put on sunscreen, it was still mid-May and the sun caressed his skin, the breeze was even a little cool, but perhaps it wasn't such a bad idea to take some precautionary measures, he again looked at the mole on his shoulder which seemed to be growing, but the more he looked at it, the more convinced he became that he was seeing things, until the next time he got undressed. Spartacus, who had taken the spot next to him, appeared in his trunks, let's see how the water is, he said, the ladies will undoubtedly dawdle for a while yet, and he strode down towards the sea on his long legs, he really was quite skinny, he didn't have a swimmer's figure, but he was quite wiry, Krustev, however, said to himself that perhaps in swim trunks he actually looked better than the young man, and strutted towards the water. He tested the foam with his toes, it was pleasant, white and soft. Spartacus warily waded in up to his ankles, it's fine, he said, what, asked Krustev, he had spaced out for a moment, listening to the rumbling of the sea, like in a seashell, he said to himself, like in a seashell, the water's warm, Spartacus declared and pitched forward, because the girls, who had snuck up behind them, were trying to knock him into the water, Krustev froze, because Sirma was topless, her brown nipples jutted up inquisitively, challenging the sun and the wind, shit, he said to himself, now I'll have to figure out how not to look at her, Maya perhaps sensed his anxiousness, because she left Sirma to horse around with Spartacus, on whom the sight clearly made no impression, and went over to him, how is it, are you happy, she asked, he was looking into the sun and he shaded his eyes with his palm, well yeah, he nodded, I'm happy and almost meant it, but only almost, because one part of him was still back at the house, the empty, sleeping house with the family portrait on the wall, with Elena in America and Irina in the graveyard, in the crumbly, drowsing dirt, which the worms wiggled out of, abruptly, rudely awakened by the shovels that came bursting in, and thought to himself that it was like an hourglass that someone was constantly turning over so that the sand moved continuously through the two glass bulbs, he poked at the sand with his thumb, remembering how as a kid he would build sandcastles with thick walls and an obligatory moat, spanned by a bridge, but the bridges often collapsed, come on, let's go in, Maya said to him and carefully waded in, in the meantime, Spartacus had fallen to his knees in the water and kept egging Sirma on, come on, push me over, now I'm your height so you've got nothing to complain about, she tried to kick him, but he grabbed her foot and she ended up in the water with a screech, is it warm, Spartacus asked, you're gonna see for yourself soon enough, Sirma threatened, I'm gonna get my revenge, just you wait. Krustev sank in up to his chest, the water really was amazingly warm and pleasant, he felt relieved, now the sand was flowing into the bright bulb, a short distance ahead of him Maya was floating on her back, Spartacus and Sirma had also started swimming and were going further out to sea, and he regretted not being able to take off with them, he was left behind, carefully watching their heads, which protruded up over the blue graveyard like exotic fruit.

[6] She let Sirma and Spartacus swim out and calmly began paddling along the beach, from time to time simply relaxing onto the water, it would look bad if all three of them rushed out to sea, while Elena's dad had to sit there and wait for them, and he was clearly worried, actually his attempt to play the fatherly role was pretty laughable, it didn't fit him, he seemed too nice to be their father, he was a musician, maybe in the business world he had learned to act older than he was, and surely it had strained his nerves, but he was interesting, not only because of his secret, which they had quickly figured out, despite the fact that he didn't want to talk about it, yes, it would be pretty absurd to pick up three hitchhikers and tell them: My wife just died. Sirma had brought it up on the ferryboat while he was gone, Maya had also noticed that he was wearing his wedding ring on his left hand, only Spartacus hadn't paid attention, as was to be expected. And now Sirma had once again put her, put them all in an awkward position with her decision to romp around the beach topless; while she was getting ready, Maya wondered what to wear, she usually went topless, too, she almost laughed out loud in the water, remembering how, the first time the two of them had come out of their tents topless, Spartacus, at the height of his testosterone-drenched teenage years, had helplessly gotten a hard-on and had tried to hide it by burying himself in the sand, but since he was so thin and bony, it was painfully obvious, it was cute, of course, he was already used to it, but now it wasn't just the three of them, they were with Elena's dad, after all, when there's

an outsider they should at least take that into consideration a little, or else maybe Sirma had gotten it in her head to hook up with him, despite the fact that he was Elena's father, or precisely because of it; but her breasts were nicer than Sirma's, Maya was quite sure of this—just as firm, but still significantly larger, weren't they, no, they weren't gigantic knockers, of course, and thank goodness for that, but they were larger.

She got out of the water a little dazed and lay down on her towel, she loved that feeling, coming out of the sea wet and letting the sun suck the moisture from your skin, drop by drop, leaving only the salt, the salty sun on her skin, but the exact nuances of that sensation had changed over the years, it had been one thing then, when she was little, she would sink onto the sand, spilling out over it, losing herself amid the countless grains, then that red shiver had appeared, the goose bumps, that warmth behind the eyelids that gradually washed over your whole body and hid between your thighs, even now it wasn't bad at all, yes, the wind was blowing, licking her moist, salty skin, then from somewhere close by she heard the rhythmic bouncing of a ball, accompanied by a shout from time to time, Maya turned over onto her stomach and lifted her head, a little way down the beach there was a volleyball court and four young men were playing, their dark, sweaty bodies glistened in the sun as if smeared with honey, she stared at their flinching, carved muscles, why not, last year on the Black Sea there'd been that cutie with the blue eyes from Serdika, she again dropped her head onto the towel and closed her eyes, the salty sun behind her eyelids, she heard footsteps nearby and sensed someone's shadow on her body. Toasting a bit, eh, said Spartacus, you didn't swim much at all, we went all the way to the buoy, where's Sirma she asked and Spartacus pointed at the sea over his shoulder, still in the water, she thinks she's a fish. Move, you're blocking my sun, she said. Spartacus toweled himself off thoroughly, but afterwards sat down right on the sand, scooped up a handful and watched the grains pouring out between his fingers. Elena's father also showed up, walking slowly with his arms crossed over his chest, his round face had lost some of its anxiousness. They had to think up something to distract him, the three of them never got tired of being together, but he would surely get bored. With a reflex already honed from communicating with men old enough for the purpose, Maya tried to imagine Boril Krustev in the role of her father. Perhaps he'd do a better job than her real one. Her parents had gotten divorced when she was fifteen, inhabiting the twilight of the *fake ninth-grade* and periodically falling into *funks*, which had seemed unique in their scope and intensity before she realized that nothing more typical could possibly happen to her, and even for her, she thought to herself now, the collisions with the *hypocrisy* of that world, which from the depths of her childhood had looked so coveted and captivating, but which later seemed so nightmarish, even they had passed considerably more easily, because she hadn't been alone, because she had had Sirma and Spartacus, then they had really begun turning into a single organism. For some unknown reason she remembered far fewer details from her second year of high school than from her first, that time got lost in some vague, rainy autumn evenings, waterlogged by the bland fluorescent lighting in the classrooms, which were completely identical and nobody could figure out why they had to move from one to the other every hour. Her classmates were already resigned to the fact that she and Spartacus were not a couple, even though they shared a desk. But, yes, it was a time when both she and Spartacus slightly envied Sirma for *getting way ahead of them* after her summer adventure, otherwise Spartacus didn't seem to be suffering at all and clearly their springtime romance had simply been an experiment which had somehow transformed into the relationship between the three of them, making their current unity possible, there was a girl in their class who was a bit of a metalhead and seemed to be giving Spartacus the eye, and Maya thought it was really funny that because of her the girl didn't dare venture close to the object of her desire, she talked to Spartacus about it once, why don't you go out with her, well, actually, I can't really imagine it, he said, scratching his head, what exactly can't you imagine, she giggled, but he explained to her in full seriousness that I can't imagine changing places and going to sit by her. She was struck by this. So does that mean you're never going to date anybody from our class? And she also asked him in complete seriousness, because the external world to a great extent still began and ended with their class, but he shrugged, they probably all want a *serious relationship*, while that doesn't really interest me, I'd rather keep things as they are now with you and Sirma. She didn't doubt that Spartacus truly took his decision as a sacrifice, although she had already understood one thing: guys are always afraid that girls want a *serious relationship* and that fear is a projection of their own desire for the same thing. Interesting, Maya wondered, staring at the sand pouring from Spartacus's hand, if things hadn't worked out this way, if their triangle didn't exist, how many serious relationships would she have gone through between her fourteenth and twentieth years? And how many of them would she have naively thought would lead to a logical marriage, however, as early as fifteen she realized that a logical marriage could also lead to a logical divorce, her parents had been together since high school, they had gotten married young, they

[73]

must be only slightly older than Krustev, and clearly their marriage had not survived beyond the withering of their youthful love, in that case it was surely preferable to get married later or not to get married at all, and can you imagine, Maya suddenly said to herself and inwardly burst out laughing, marrying Spartacus, but they had better first become politicians and take control of the government so as to allow marriages between three people and issue a decree in support of fornication. Around the time she started high school, when she became a *fake*, she started drawing certain conclusions and suspecting that her mother was having an affair, there were those hushed phone conversations, business trips and cold silences in the living room, and Maya instinctively took her father's side, even though, thinking back on it logically, he surely was having an affair, too, at that time. By the end of the summer, her father and mother avoided sitting down at the table together and she was sure that if they had had the space at home and an extra room, her father would have moved out of the nuptial bed (but why her father, actually, why shouldn't her mother be the one to move out?). And in the end the evening rolled around when she came home from school and caught sight of her brother watching cartoons on TV, she suddenly felt a rush of affection, he was still a kid, he had no idea what he was in for, she sat down by him and they watched cartoons together, where are Mom and Dad, she asked and he shrugged and said there's a note in the kitchen saying they're going out and will be back around eight-thirty, Maya was quite surprised, because the last thing she would've expected her parents to do at that point was to go out together, but, as it turns out, they wanted to sit down in neutral territory, at some nearby restaurant and, with the help of a nice dinner, admit that there was no point in being together anymore and that yes, the kids were already old enough, they would understand . . . Maya made sand-wiches for herself and her brother and sent him off to play on the computer, while she sat down to read, she had started in on *Tender Is the Night*, now there's another ruined marriage for you, but at least her mother wasn't crazy or at least not that much, she jumped when she heard the click of the key in the lock and went to meet the awkward expressions pasted to her parents' faces, her brother ran up and asked them where they had been, but they asked instead whether he and Maya had eaten, praised her for the sand-wiches, went into the living room and began coughing nervously. Okay, they're going to tell us now that they're getting a divorce, Maya thought, and froze in absurd, anxious expectation, as if she were about to witness some extremely solemn, holy ritual, and indeed, they clearly had decided to do it, they started out with some general chitchat, beating around the bush and surely-you've-noticed, well yes, they had noticed, Maya thought to herself, they had even discussed it and her brother really was only a child, but he was old enough to understand. At a certain moment, every-thing hung in an abrupt pause. Then her father started in again, you are both old enough, I think you'll understand, actually, her mother finished off in a tired voice, your father and I are thinking of getting a divorce. The lack of drama was shocking. In films, in books, people suffered, broke down, screamed and smashed china. But this wasn't a film, nor a book, this was real life, colorless and dull, and the sacred ritual crumbled to the floor like dust, the earth did not tremble and the world did not blaze up in supernatural conflagration, their parents looked at them helplessly and Maya, too, could not find anything to say, while her brother shifted his gaze between the three of them, unfairly thrust by their silence into a position which he should never have had to be in at all, finally he got up and with a slightly quavering voice said well, I already knew you were gonna get divorced, it's not news to me, for your information, so fine, if that's what you want, go ahead and get divorced, so be it. *So be it,* he must have gotten that from some film about epic battles and wise sorcerers.

Sirma showed up with her nipples. You're gonna grow flippers, Spartacus said. Maya was watching Krustev, he was obviously trying not to stare at Sirma's tits, wondering where to look and in the end his gaze found refuge in hers, and then, when their eyes met, his suddenly became impenetrable, until that moment this man had seemed quite simple, gloomy, suffering and sweetly uncertain, but now all of that suddenly disappeared, the warm dusk of his brown eyes stepped aside and in its place something emerged that could only be called nothingness. The nothingness had captured those exhausted, melancholy, slightly elongated Slavic eyes, but her father had a Slavic girlfriend, too, he lived with her now, and from the very beginning Maya had taken it as a double betrayal, a Slav of all things, what did these Slavic women have that made them so much better than her mother, and even Maya herself, she thought of Elena again, it was impossible not to think of Elena as she looked at her father, and in the end she looked away, so as not to think about Elena, but she kept thinking and remembered how when they were both little, her parents had treated her friend with some reserve, yes, now she very clearly recalled her mother once telling her that Elena was half Slav and to Maya that had seemed very strange, how could you be *half* something, apples could be divided in half with a knife, peaches only when you twisted them, as long as you were lucky, but even then the halves were still more or less identical, perhaps with slightly different outlines, but with the same taste in any case, so what was this mysterious half of

Elena that was so different from the other one? She watched her friend with curiosity as she carefully wrote out her letters in her notebook, looking for some kind of visible difference in the two halves of her face, but when they sat together at their desk, she could usually only see one side of her, while when they stood up, Elena's face suddenly evened out and became as normal as can be, but for a long time Maya was convinced that in those instants when she could not see her, the left half of her friend's face was different from the right, that it was *Slavic*, whatever that might mean; later she came to understand what this meant, and also that this halving of Elena was not visible to the naked eye, and surely then she had buried her silly childhood fantasy so deeply that now she was suddenly shaken by the memory, at once happy and frightened, like a prospector who has glimpsed a shiny gold flake amid the pebbles in his sieve; but now her father was living with a Slav and Maya mused that if they were to have a child, which was not completely out of the question after all, it, too, would be a *half*-Slav and what's more, it would also be her *half*-brother or sister, and for an instant she was stunned by this play of halves, after which she felt ashamed, as always happened when she caught herself thinking stupid things, and besides, she was mature enough, and the times had changed enough as well, to not pay so much attention to who in Thrace had Slavic, Illyrian, or Macedonian roots; the Dacians, of course, were another question entirely.

The sun was already clearly setting and all at once it grew cold; Sirma went over to the tent and finally threw on a T-shirt. They sat for a while longer on the beach and Krustev, suddenly chipper, told them about his first trip to Thasos, he had been seventeen and was playing in a band called Stinkweed, his first more-or-less serious band, he, of course, was the youngest, they set off hitching en masse and made it to Thasos, back then things were completely different, this campground didn't exist at all, there was another one, totally primitive, but that was all they needed, back then they were living in a different world and didn't even notice the sand beneath their feet, one evening they ended up as part of a big gang gathered at the port, somebody shoved a guitar in his hands and he started playing; as he told the story, clearly his pride was struggling with his desire to play it down; the guitar belonged to an elderly fisherman from Thasos, who finally went over to him, grasped him firmly by the shoulder, looked sharply into his eyes and snapped: The guitar is yours, my boy. He tried to object, after all, he already had an electric guitar at home, but the fisherman would hear none of it, he just kept repeating she's yours, but you had better play her only when you're near the sea, and the seventeen-year-old Krustev gave in. Over the next few years, whenever he set out for the seaside, he always took the fisherman's guitar with him, then brought it back home and didn't dare play it so far inland, but once he said to himself come on, what's the big deal, he was at his place with friends, he grabbed the guitar, but she wouldn't obey, she resisted, he tried to force her, Maya liked the eroticism in the way he put it, and in the end he broke a string, then he got scared, set her aside and didn't change the string; and so for twenty years now he'd been keeping that guitar with the broken string. Maya imagined how at the instant when the string snapped, far from the guitar, perhaps out on the open sea, the fisherman suddenly collapsed onto the deck of his boat and died. It all sounded like something from a novel, there was a Macedonian author who wrote stuff like that and Maya suspected that Krustev was making it up, but even if that were the case, it was still a good story. Sirma and Spartacus also looked impressed. You and I have got a lot of talking to do about music, Spartacus remarked and satisfaction visibly washed over Krustev's face. Sirma got up, stood on her tiptoes and stretched her arms up, raising her t-shirt and revealing her ass in her tight-fitting bikini bottoms. I say we go get a drink, she suggested. A mojito would do me some good right about now. Ouzo, Krustev countered with a smile. Ouzo, mojito, pick your poison, Sirma said.

Only a disheveled foreign couple was sitting at the wooden bar, drinking beer. The guy had a shaved head, was shirtless and had a little dragon tattooed on his shoulder, while dark-blonde, very well-done dreads stuck out of the girl's head, on her ankle, perched on a rung of the high stool, she wore a big blue clay anklet. Maya decided they were Germans, but soon she heard the buzz-cut desperately repeating *pommes frites, pommes frites* to the girl behind the bar, the brunette was looking at him with a patient smile, Maya went over and explained French fries, ohhh, the bartender said, thanks, the guy and the girl turned their heads towards her at the same time, staring, you speak French, uh yeah, Maya said, we're sitting over there, Spartacus, who didn't like chatting with random tourists beyond his professional duties, nudged her side, I'll be there in a second, Maya told him, but the French couple were so excited by their find that they drowned her in a stream of words. Nobody speaks French here, the girl complained, and our English isn't that great, Maya agreed, you're right, French people don't come here too often so the locals don't usually speak French, however, the guy started explaining that they had been traveling around the region for two weeks now, they had arrived in Thasos only last night, and everywhere it had been really hard to get by with French. He was already a little drunk, he was talking loudly and quickly, they'd started their trip in Ephesus in Lydia, all the stone shit there was really cool, the girl with the dreads chipped in, yeah, the guy agreed, we had a great time in Lydia and after just a week we even started picking up some of the language, you know, a word here and a word there and it works out and you say to yourself cool, now in Phrygia it's gonna be even easier to get around—yeah, right!—fucking Phrygian is completely different, even the fucking alphabet is different, so I tell them, you use the Macedonian alphabet, and they get all offended, oh come on, it's not Macedonian, it's from Chios, right, 'cause it was supposedly thought up by some St. Whoever-the-hell from the island of Chios, I can't even fucking pronounce it—he imitated the velar "ch" as if choking—and so the Macedonians, right, they supposedly got it from the Phrygians: totally fucked up! Well, that's what I've heard, too, Maya smiled. Well, we'll go to Macedonia, too, the girl shrugged, to see what they'll tell us there. So here we are now in Thasos, in this Thrace of yours, the Frenchman with the dragon on his shoulder continued heatedly, and your language doesn't have a damn thing in common with Lydian, nor with Phrygian, for fuck's sake, I can't understand you people, why the hell do you need all these different languages? Maya started getting annoyed, well, then why is French so different from German, she asked, but they just stared at her in confusion, well, 'cause we're different nations, the guy said, well, okay then, so we and the Phrygians and the Lydians are different nations, too, Maya laughed, but the guy kept stubbornly insisting, what's so different about you, he kept protesting, I can't see any difference at all, you've divided yourselves up into a pile of countries and on top of everything, every county has this or that minority, Slavs in Thrace, Thracians in Illyria, I don't know what they have in Phrygia, Patagonians, maybe, and everybody speaks a different fucking language, but at least here you all use a normal alphabet, he added as a compliment, sensing, perhaps, that he was starting to get carried away.

Maya mentally noted how lucky it was that none of the others spoke French, the bald guy really was pretty drunk and quite sincerely indignant over the fact that in the different countries nearby there were different peoples who spoke different languages, we're just getting totally confused, said the girl with the dreads in a diplomatic attempt to put an end to the topic and fortunately the black-haired bartender reappeared with their French fries. Maya went back to the others, who were already drinking: Krustev— ouzo, Spartacus—beer, Sirma—a mojito; she ordered a mojito as well from the black-haired bartender and settled onto the stool, what were you talking about, Sirma baited her, I was arguing with the bald guy, Maya said, about whether his basic problem was being drunk or being stupid. Still I wonder, she thought to herself, how things were during the Macedonian Empire, everybody was part of the same country, yet they were still different peoples, back then that poor French guy would've been even more confused, since he wouldn't even have had the basic signpost of national borders, incidentally, European travelers had come back then as well to map the different ethnic groups, Spartacus had told her—he was interested in history—how all of their maps were completely different, in the center of Seuthopolis there was a street named after an Austrian ethnographer, whose map showed the Thracians occupying nearly the whole Balkan Peninsula with the exception of old Hellas, while according to Spartacus in Illyrian cities they named their streets after another ethnographer, an Italian, whose map had spread the ink-blotch of their ethnicity all the way to the delta of the Danube. Maya imagined the Austrian and the Italian yanking each other's beards and furiously tearing up the painstakingly painted maps. Afterwards, after the Macedonian inheritance had been divided up, every nation had waved the corresponding map, drawn by some European sympathizer, and thanks to those maps they had waged far too many wars, but hey, the Frenchman with the little dragon was right that there were still minorities of the neighboring peoples left in every country. The mojito smelled cool and crisp, and Maya gazed at the freshly cut mint in satisfaction. They make a mean cocktail here, believe you me, Sirma noted, and that's not all, yeah, Spartacus chimed in, they have sex on the beach and triple orgasm, Krustev started laughing, sex on the beach, Sirma said, I could do that by myself, and immediately corrected herself, well, not exactly by myself, but I sure wouldn't need a bartender. Yeah, but Spartacus likes the bartender chick, Maya teased him, and he went along with it, man, I was so nervous, he said, I knew I should ask for something way more chichi, but what do I end up ordering—one pathetic little beer. Elena's father was sitting at the end, listening to them kidding around and smiling. This is where it's at, Maya said to herself.

She again stared at the little mint leaves and asked herself how their trio must look in the older man's eyes. While driving through the Rhodopes, he had asked them, so do you do everything together, after which he seemed to have decided not to wonder and to calmly accept every side of their unusual relationship that they decided to show him. Maya mentally noted the fact that their relationship could still (or perhaps now?) be called *unusual*. She wasn't even totally sure how much outsiders considered it unusual, because practically speaking no one knew enough, of course, no one else had experienced the things the three of them had experienced together, and since no one knew them to the degree to which they knew one another, no one could say whether all that was unusual or not. Not counting the Elena fiasco, she had avoided bringing her other more or less random friends to hang out with Spartacus and Sirma, the two of them also didn't bring other people in; way back when, Sirma had warned them other people wouldn't understand in any case and would just ask annoying questions, so they were better off not creating such headaches for themselves in the first place. As far as guys were concerned, Maya liked hanging out with big mixed groups from time to time, she liked detaching herself from Spartacus and Sirma and sitting around drinking beer with guys who were so different from her, who so rarely thought about their own bodies, who acted so simply and effectively, like some eager and well-oiled machines. She liked flirting, and when the guys had a knack for it, too, sometimes she would hook up with them, and sometimes these hook-ups resulted in *near-relationships*, she would suddenly start to feel light, ethereal, as if about to take flight if she didn't hold the guy's hand, for example, with that Dobrin, whom she had, in fact, gone with for a dozen days after Elena's party, he was husky, yet his muscles were devoid of aggression, somehow staid and calmly confident of their strength, and that, combined with his shaggy hair and chestnut beard, really made him look like a good-natured bear. He was slow and passive like a swollen river, he didn't expect anything and was ready to accept whatever life offered him. Maya saw him around on the streets and in cafes after they had officially decided that they weren't together. He would give her a friendly smile and she was sure that his ursine river was flowing as calmly and gently as ever through thick Slavic forests filled with wooly elms and raspberries twinkling amid the greenery. For example, Maya didn't know whether it was *unusual* that she felt no desire to tie herself down to some man, to live with him and to start a family, whether the feeling of family she got from Sirma and Spartacus was *unusual*, a family with the strict ritual of the mysteries, in which it was possible, as it surely was in all families, to bicker and be jealous, to kick up a fight sometimes, and in the end to have that not lead to anything that might destroy the balance between the three corners of the triangle. But now she was looking at Elena's father, the thick, wiry stubble jabbing into his cheeks, the bags under his eyes, a forty-something man, next to him Spartacus was still a boy, and she wondered whether all of that would be possible when they were forty-something, too, or whether it would remain as some odd-romantic memory of youth, like his story about the guitar that he should play only by the sea. She couldn't imagine it, however, which likely meant that it wouldn't happen.

She stirred the green coolness in her glass distractedly and rejoined the others' conversation, Spartacus had kept his promise to grill Krustev about music and the two of them radiated infantile satisfaction while discussing the solo in "Stargazer"; in all of her musical conversations with Spartacus, with which their friendship had, in fact, begun, Maya had never managed to talk like that and she began to suspect that there was something typically male going on here which was foreign to her and which seemed slightly pointless, the ability to listen to the instruments separately, to articulate and compare them, she simply liked certain songs and never felt any need to analyze them, still it was good that Spartacus couldn't actually play an instrument, because then his conversations with Krustev surely would have turned into complete musician-speak, she had once found herself in the middle of a drummers' rap session and her ears rang with downbeats and off-beats, double-bass, high-hats and asymmetrical meters, and she had decided that playing music was far more boring than listening to it. Krustev had suddenly become confident and calm, with the satisfaction of a dedicated teacher who has found himself an alert and responsive student. Maya liked such teachers, even if they weren't artistic like Krustev, but most of all she liked the old-fashioned, balding professors who wore suits, spoke slowly and clearly, and carefully wiped their fragile glasses with a little cloth from time to time; she also liked the smell of dust and wood in the lecture halls, the turbid yellowish light in the high, vaulted corridors and all the rituality of the university; yet it lacked something which even the crappiest high school possessed: life together, the aggregate of all the students, divided into class periods and breaks, that reassuringly shared gossip mill, where everyone knew everyone else and there was no need to make plans by phone, since they would meet thanks to a necessity that had fused with habit to such an extent that it looked like the natural state of things. And, of course, when they went to college, they all already had their established friendships, their networks of people and places, and they weren't particularly interested in forming new ones, and even when that nevertheless happened, it never happened in that spontaneous, imperceptible way devoid of purpose and intention in whcih relationships in high school had sprouted up. If she hadn't met Spartacus and Sirma in high school, back in the days when she was a *fake*, it would never have been possible to meet them later and in some other place. She slurped the last drops of the mojito noisily through the straw and her nostrils took in the next scent wafting from the dive at the edge of the campgrounds, the smell of fish, the salty and sizzling scent of simple wooden tables with paper tablecloths and of a noisy twilight in which silverware and laughter jangled. She looked at Sirma, who bared her teeth in a smile, I know what you're thinking, she said, I'm hungry, too.

[7] Everyone was drowning here, he was surrounded by drowned fruit flies and other little bugs, and he was swimming, swimming away, so as not to drown, but at a certain point he reached the clear wall of the glass and could go no further, he couldn't hang on to it, because he didn't have vacuum feet like the flies, which, by the way, also weren't able to hang on to the glass, wet and disheveled, they could only go back to the center or wander the outlying districts, along the periphery of the glass wall, but the important thing was not to stop swimming in the strange liquid with its undefined color and smell, flat beer or cold tea, from time to time new gnats would arrive from outside and would sink into the liquid with an inexplicable urge towards self-sacrifice, kicking their little legs, trying to flap their stuck-together wings, but they would soon drop lifelessly into the glass. Spartacus wondered how he had ended up here and what would happen if someone decided to drink the liquid, he already felt a traitorous exhaustion in his muscles, he couldn't keep swimming forever, even if only in some glass, and completely businesslike, without fear, he thought to himself that in the end he, too, would surely drown like all the other bugs, but suddenly it hit him that he could float on his back and relax, he tried it and wouldn't you know, it worked, his body submissively went slack in the liquid and for some time there was nothing.

But then a brrrm-zhhhush-zoop started up, obviously some fly, not a fruit fly, but some bigger one had slipped out of the glass with him and was now ramming the netted corners of the tent, let's have a brrrm now for Mom, a zhhhush for Dad, a zoop for Grandma and Grandpa, okay, the fly obediently carried out the instructions, keeping up the rhythm and, as annoying as it was, Spartacus was thankful for it because they were moving after all, cutting a trail through the forest together, he carefully pushed aside the branches, brrrm-zhhhush-zoop and at one point, so late that he felt ashamed of his own foolishness, he realized that this was no fly, but *the writer with the Caucasian Ford*, the humming and buzzing were coming from the engine, and there was no forest anywhere nearby, nor any glass of cold tea, the old, decrepit car puttered along the rural route, I've written two novels and thrrrrreee! collections of poetry, the fly said and Spartacus suddenly realized that he had read one of those two novels, he now remembered it perfectly clearly, it was called *Ascension Day* and in it one of his classmates axe-murdered the girl he was in love with, until now, however, Spartacus had thought that the novel was by Leo Tolstoy, but now he realized that, in fact, it was by the windbag with the Caucasian Ford, he was impressed, then confused, so how did he know it was his book, since the guy hadn't said anything about his novel, not even the title, but still he knew it, he knew it instinctively, the way he knew not to touch a hot stove, so, he asked, you know my classmates? I don't know them, the guy replied, buuut! art moves in mysterious ways, and I mean mysterious with a capital M! Now Spartacus was holding the novel itself on his lap, paging through it and instead of letters he saw scenes from it before his eyes as if he were present at the events, at the same time he also saw the windbag writing the novel and wanted to shout at him, what are you doing, keep your hands on the wheel, but the guy had fallen into some kind of blissful, artistic trance, his hand raced over the pages that Spartacus was simultaneously reading, the windbag turned to him and asked should I tell you how it ends, no, Spartacus replied indignantly, why would you tell me, well, because, the windbag replied, if I don't tell you, we'll crash. But Spartacus stubbornly refused, he didn't want him to give away the ending, he wanted to find out for himself, to see the final scene projected like a hologram from the book on his lap, the windbag shrugged, let go of the wheel and they really did crash instantly.

Now the important thing is to fall asleep, Spartacus told himself, if I fall asleep the car will start moving again. But he never figured out whether he managed to fall asleep or not, in any case the car was no longer there and he was completely convinced that he was in his tent, to make sure he even flipped through some of what had happened that day, yes, exactly, Elena's dad had picked them up, they had taken the ferryboat to Thasos, they had gone swimming, drunk beer, eaten dinner, afterwards they all had felt really tired and had gone to bed, now he was furious that he couldn't fall asleep properly, this night was his chance, they had gone to bed so early, when would he have a chance to sleep the following nights, some pachanga would start up, Sirma topless with a lei of Hawaiian flowers around her neck, now the petals of the flowers covered her nipples, but the more he looked at her, the more he realized that the flowers were, in fact, growing, multiplying and taking over an ever-larger part of her body, this was happening slowly and she didn't seem to notice it, she kept dancing some strange dance, look, Maya told him and squeezed his hand, look, the flowers will erase her, he again tried to shout to warn her, but he only heard some mooing in his ears, while the fly stirred again, brrrm-zhhhush-zoop, and besides the fly he heard very clearly someone walking around outside his tent, sniffing and wheezing, was that a dog, could somebody steal his backpack, somebody walking around his tent with a dog? Zoop, said the fly. It wasn't a fly, it was the zipper of his tent. Spartacus struggled to get up, but his body was terribly heavy, he couldn't even move his arm. Zoop, and a little later zoop again, and female laughter. That was

Sirma's sister, he was absolutely convinced of this, true, Sirma had never mentioned having a sister, but now it was as clear as day to him that this was Sirma's sister, they looked alike, but this girl was somehow softer and smiling, she was kneeling in the sand in front of his tent and quickly pulling the zipper up and down, now showing her face, now hiding it, she was playing with the zipper and laughing, Sirma's sister. Suddenly the whirr of the zipper stopped and for a long time there was nothing again.

He woke up once and for all from the heat. The sun had clearly climbed high enough to warm the tent and it was gradually becoming a greenhouse inside. But he didn't feel like getting out. If the sun was already high in the sky, then he'd slept a long time. He could still remember most of the strange dreams he'd had, it must've been really stuffy, and a fat black fly was crawling over the netting of the tent. But the zipper of the tent was sitting there, quietly closed. Sirma's sister. He felt his cock apathetically harden in the usual morning erection, that tiresome caprice of the hormones. He suddenly realized who the girl from his dream had been, hidden behind the inexplicable idea that Sirma had a sister. She was a girl from high school, younger than they were, whose birthday party they had ended up at more or less accidentally a year ago, they were already in college, but they still had friends in high school and the latter had dragged them to some party. Spartacus snorted, that was surely his last true *high school* stunt. He knew the girl in passing, who, in fact, did not particularly resemble Sirma, but she was attractive, still he had gone to the party without any plans, but gradually and imperceptibly he had had way too much to drink, so much so that he blacked out and whatever he knew about that evening had come from Sirma and Maya's giggling stories. He wondered how much to believe them, because he had a hard time believing that in his drunkenness he had been so hyperactive so as to do everything they had attributed to him. According to them, he was racing around everywhere, he had chased a solitary and sullen skinhead, insisting that he explain exactly what his problem with blacks was, he was the life of the party until at one point he definitively homed in on the birthday girl, dancing a slow dance with her, the song ended, but they kept spinning around, staggering in the middle of the room, Spartacus perhaps remembered that vaguely when they told him, a soft, dazed spinning around the girl's warm breath, and the realization that he couldn't see anything, who knows what kind of alcohol they had foisted on him, but the next part he really didn't remember: according to Sirma and Maya everyone in the room was laughing loudly, shouting at them that the song was over and it was time to finally untangle themselves, but they kept spinning, so finally one girl said well, let's not let a good dance go to waste and sat down at the piano, that sounded believable, because there really had been a piano in the room, and so the girl had started playing another ballad on the piano and they kept spinning for a while longer, and when it finished, Spartacus and the girl as if on command tumbled under the piano and started vigorously making out. Here Spartacus had tossed back his head and started laughing in disbelief, indignant and satisfied, now you're making stuff up, he kept saying, even though that could've been true, too, he had some memory of the warm taste of the girl's mouth, of her busy tongue, while Sirma and Maya swore they weren't embellishing a single detail, well, if that's how it was, he shrugged, that makes it even funnier, it's just too bad that I clearly had no idea what was going on, so you were having fun without me. In any case, it was true that in the morning or some time around then, he woke up in a huge bed in which five people were sleeping or pretending to sleep, the birthday girl was snuggled up to him and looked extremely out of it, he tried to kiss her, so that thing about the piano must've been true, otherwise why would he have done that, but she couldn't even move, she merely looked at him numbly, they really must have drunk some very sketchy alcohol, lift your head a little, he said jokingly, but she replied I can't, I'll throw up in your mouth, and shortly thereafter she cleared out, maybe she really was going to throw up, however, there were two other girls in the bed, they looked pretty young, but he played dumb, putting his arms around one of them and lying down comfortably, she gave in to his embrace, without saying anything, but also without moving closer, and at one point he woke up or sobered up or enough of both to ask himself what the hell am I doing here, he removed his hand from the random body he had come across, got up and went to splash cold water on his face, but in the kitchen Sirma and Maya, who were drinking coffee, met him with a round of applause, and shortly thereafter dragged him outside to go home, the first buses were already lazily humming in the darkness.

Spartacus stepped out of his tent and the day sprawled before him, plentiful and yellow, and the seconds, milliseconds and the other finer beats of time stuck to his legs, as he waded through the day with Maya and Sirma, and with that strange, sad person who had suddenly hit the road, only to wake up the husband of a dead wife and the father of an ex-lover, ex-friend, ex-threat. All four of them lazily watched the sand from the glass upper globe slip into the lower one, Spartacus continued running various memories through his head, as he had done for most of the previous day while they were in the car, and at one point he wondered if he hadn't changed places with Elena's father, who certainly had more right than he did to dig through his memories and pay so much attention to them, and perhaps to sit here on this island beach and to look out at the sea with the feeling that everything that was going to happen had already happened. But Sirma and Maya had also gone silent, sunk into themselves, mulling various things over, as if they, too, inhabited some previous stories, perhaps at the end of the day everything was due to Elena, to her invisible yet tangible presence ever since they had gotten into her father's car, had she ridden in it recently, had she seeped into the seats like a scent, like an infection, she really had a knack for being present, for hovering nearby, even when she was thousands of miles away, maybe she had also captured their minds in some way, forcing them to race down the steep slope of memory, but perhaps in the end there really wasn't much of anything that could happen here, on this island, on this sandy beach, in front of the greedy maw of the sea, which fawned in the surf and licked at their toes.

His romance with Elena had lasted less than a month. Their bodies had raged in a staggering frenzy, they had kissed furiously in the middle of the street, she had bitten his lips as he pressed her to the façade of public buildings downtown, sometimes the doormen would come out and chase them away, not so much angry as amused, they would take off and Elena would whisper in his ear, *did you see that, the doorman had a hard-on*, and he would go crazy again, seized by the thought of the hard, grinning doorman in his blue uniform, they would sink into the park somewhere, into its wooded part, throwing themselves on the ground and unbuttoning their clothes with trembling fingers. Afterwards, tamed for a few hours, they would find Sirma and Maya, who eyed them mockingly, timidly or with outright hostility, so are you screwing them, too, Elena had asked him at the very beginning and he laughed, it wasn't the first time he'd heard that question, others usually asked which of the two he was sleeping with, and he would put that topic to bed once and for all by saying both, and even though it wasn't true in the literal sense of the word, it was nevertheless the truth in its own, uh, metaphysical way. But when Elena had asked him so are you screwing them, too, he had hesitated as to what to answer and his hesitation had lasted long enough for her to decide that that, his hesitation, was the answer and that in that case she could choose to believe whatever she wanted, and she had chosen to believe that yes, the three of them indulged in wild orgies, and she had started telling him what nice breasts Maya had, how much she liked Sirma's green eyes, he had thrown her onto the couch in the sleeping office, which her father had given her the key to, stripped her and rushed into her, to make her shut up, but once, when they were doing it, she had again begun fantasizing out loud about the girls, how nice it would be if they were here, too, she had said it like that, kneeling on the couch, he had covered her mouth with his hand and pulled her towards him, her body twisted and trembled, she bellowed, but he pressed her mouth tightly with his hand and didn't let go until he had come as well, at which point he groaned you're crazy, but she just smiled exultantly and said: Aren't I, though? They didn't see each other for the next three days because her parents had made her go with them somewhere on a long weekend. Without meaning to, Spartacus glanced at her father, rather ridiculous in his black swim trunks, just as all older men looked ridiculous in their swim trunks for some inexplicable reason, even though he was still in good shape, he didn't have a gut, yet the first premonition of old age hovered around his body, it wasn't a mark on the skin, it wasn't a wrinkle or something visible, but Krustev seemed to exude his own uneasiness, his reduced sense of comfort in his own body, or at least that's how it seemed to him, the girls surely were of another mind entirely, he had long since realized that they saw older men in a different light, he thought about him driving the red car which had brought them here or maybe some other car, a previous one, and next to him was his wife, who was now dead, and in the backseat was Elena and she was replaying dirty scenes in her mind and she smelled of sex, of him, of the couch in the office and the cool dirt under the spruces in the park, he couldn't imagine those people together, he didn't see anything in common between that fury in the body of the half-Slavic girl and the anxious man who looked as if he had been cold for a long time and was now gradually beginning to feel the rays of sunlight on his skin, and he felt a deep thankfulness that Krustev didn't know what he had done with his daughter, although on the other hand he had surely been wondering about it the whole time, surely all fathers were like that and he would become that way, too, if he had a daughter, sometimes he thought abstractly about some other time and place in which he would have a family and children, but in these visions, too, he could not solve the problem of who, in fact, would be the mother of his children, couldn't the kids somehow be born without a mother, while he would stay with Sirma and Maya, or else perhaps he would have one child with each of them, that was now possible, and all thanks to Elena, wasn't that right. While she had been on that long weekend with her parents, the three of them had gone out alone and he had thought that everything would be as usual, since they had learned to leave their hook-ups and relationships, insofar as they existed, aside and not to let them into their triangle, he didn't feel like he had let Elena inside and hadn't even thought about it, but Maya and Sirma, it seemed, had another opinion on the matter, they were mad at him, they sipped their beer and let fly snide comments meant to insult him, what the hell is your problem, he asked angrily, we don't have a problem, Sirma declared, you're the one with a problem in your head, and not your big one, but your little one. He got up and stalked across the lawn with long strides, but behind his back he could hear Sirma yelling after him, now there, don't you see, he felt offended by their unfairness, especially by Maya, who had spun 180 degrees, hadn't she been the one who had brought her friend and had wanted them to buddy up to her, and in the beginning Sirma had been angry with her, while he had defended her, he didn't understand what the two of them wanted from him, yes, maybe things between Elena and him were more serious than with his previous girlfriends, than with Sirma and Maya's guys, but he hadn't expected such jealousy and it all seemed incredibly irrational, absurd and childish, which, he thought to himself now, perhaps it really had been.

When they again hopped over to the bar, because in the end there wasn't much else to do between the sea and the campground fence, on the coarse sand that unexpectedly flowed into the dry soil beneath tall, straight pines, so strange and uncharacteristic of the seaside, Krustev again insisted on treating them and they took him up on it, each time they put up less of a fight, the man obviously enjoyed doing it, while for them every free round was a breath of fresh air. In the car, Maya had told him that they'd taken the year off to think about whether they really wanted to study what they were studying, and that was true, but only almost. In fact, it was Maya who had taken a year off not just because of that, but because she needed money, after the divorce both her mother and her father's finances were not exactly rosy, while her brother was growing and eating a lot, at least that's what Maya said, half-joking, half-serious, but on the other hand, she could translate and teach French without taking a year off her major, so the idea of taking a step back and reflecting on things really was important, in any case she had suggested it and he and Sirma had taken her up on it, because it had seemed wise to them, they wouldn't lose anything by doing something else for a year, and in any case Spartacus was growing ever more skeptical where law was concerned, while Sirma, who had gone to fantastic lengths to get into her dream major of architecture, was simply furious about the way the teachers blocked their students' progress so they couldn't become competition. The year would soon come full circle and they had to decide what to do from then on, but for now they could still travel, think, and earn some money with which to think and travel. Spartacus calculated that if things went on like this, even if they extended their vacation, he might still have some money left over when they got back. He had set aside the payment from the last brochure, and now, of course, tourist season was starting and there would be work, new groups of German grannies and Mesozoic Americans. His own grandmother, from the village near the Sea of Marmara, always loved to say that easy money was the most fun to spend. Now, having earned a little something and despite the fact that he still lived with his parents, he no longer asked for an allowance, Spartacus was convinced that his grandmother was dead wrong: it was the most fun to spend money you earned yourself and which you knew you'd put time and energy into, which you were now free to squander in one fell swoop, getting your revenge on the tourists by turning them into beer and fried fish, draining them and gnawing them down to the bone, or better yet, transforming a glossy brochure into a concert ticket, watching for an hour and a half as the smoke of your burning cash envelops the musicians on stage, watching with delight as the time-turned-to-sound breaks loose and flies off. He didn't like carrying cash, no matter how little, he hurried to turn it into other things, and sometimes he wondered what in the world he would do if some day he made a lot of money, say what Krustev made, it seemed logical, maybe he, too, would take a shine to some kids who reminded him of his own youth and would pick up their tab, but Krustev, with his promoter's agency, at whose concerts Spartacus had turned his cash to smoke and time to sound, and with his stores for home entertainment systems, that Krustev was probably too rich to be able to squander his money, he didn't have enough time. No matter how egotistical it was, there was something deeply pointless, some insult to being itself, in dying without having relieved yourself of that burden. Once, only once, had Spartacus ended up without a single cent, he had been maybe seventeen, he was going to meet Sirma and Maya on the bridge over the Tonzos, they were late and for lack of anything better to do, Spartacus dug into his pocket and found only a small coin, it wasn't even enough for ice cream, so he raised his arm and chucked it far into the river; cars whizzed past on both sides of the bridge, it was noisy and he didn't hear it splash into the river, but he told himself, okay, now I don't have a single cent in my pocket, and he felt an incredible rush of freedom. He spent three days like that, until the next installment from his parents, of course, that was easy at seventeen, what do you really need to buy, when it comes to beer in the park, there was always someone willing to cough up cash for it instead of you, and if nobody does, then you go without beer, but despite that for those three days he completely consciously lived the joy of the penniless, looking to spend most of his time out and about, wandering through the streets, looking in the shop windows and feeling pride and relief that he could not buy himself anything whatsoever, not even a bottle of water. He knew, with that knowledge which stands in the corner like a heavy block of stone that you can't budge, that those three days would never repeat themselves. The older he got, the more doomed he was to earn money and spend it, spinning his toothy gears in the machine of exchange, grinding coins in his molars.

[8] Sirma was lying on the bunk of the ferryboat from Thessaloniki to Rhodes, bored. The others were bored up in the fresh air, looking out at the sea, but she was already sick of that. The sea didn't change much. From time to time they would see some larger island, or else just naked rock, carelessly tossed in the middle of the watery desert, but the islands, too, looked so much alike that after the first few, gawking at them wasn't particularly interesting. At first, Sirma had imagined that the twenty-four-hour voyage at sea would be exciting. Maybe it would be exciting at the end: the gradual approach towards their goal, maneuvers for entering the harbor, the shrill siren; but until then there wasn't much to do. But then again, there hadn't been much to do on Thasos either, despite the beautiful sand, which so unexpectedly flowed into the dry soil beneath the pines, their asses had started itching from the sand and they had wanted to hit the road again, Krustev in any case had suggested they go to Rhodes, and with their already weakened resistance, they had let him buy the tickets and explain that he wasn't doing it to flaunt how much money he had, but simply because he felt like traveling and he liked the company, which still didn't sound so great, because it turned out that he was

buying himself fellow travelers, but how could you get mad at the guy, he was too sad to get mad at and besides, he was cool, in his own way. Maya ducked into the cabin, raised her eyebrows when she saw Sirma lying there and asked her if she felt seasick. She wasn't seasick, the ferry was big and steady. I was just lying here thinking, she said, and at one point I realized: I'm just lying here. Maya had come back to get her camera to take pictures from the deck, Sirma admired her enthusiasm. She went out, leaving Sirma alone again. Always the three of them, just the three of them, but a person still needs to be alone from time to time. And perhaps there wouldn't even be that *three of them*, if she hadn't insisted on it back then, if she hadn't stubbornly and purposefully woven their shared garment out of myriad opportunities and occasions, because it could also be otherwise, because they could have each set out on their own path, which, at the end of the day, is the custom among people, and they could have started living like everyone else. Yes, all three of them wanted to be a threesome, but someone had to make the effort so it would happen, and she was that someone. Two incidents had convinced her that that was the best variant, that they would do well in creating such solid ties that no one could come between them, first that stupid incident at the seaside, when she'd lost her virginity, she laughed out loud remembering Maya's bewildered look when she'd said *we fucked*, the truth was she had gotten almost no pleasure out of the sex itself, the satisfaction came from what she was inflicting on her body, from grabbing it and offering it like a piece of meat to that idiot to poke and jab, she liked that supremacy over the body, the pain, the greasy stream of blood that trickled between her legs and she was even sorry that she would not be able to inflict the same thing in all its glory on herself a second time. Maybe she didn't actually like sex. And maybe, not maybe but surely she was frightened by her masochistic pleasure, which had nothing to do with the nerve endings in the clitoris that she had read about in books with titles like *I'm Becoming a Woman*, and, in fact, she had run away to Maya and Spartacus, set them up around herself for protection, so as to be part of something bigger and thus to be less herself, because the truth was she didn't like herself, didn't know herself and didn't know what she was capable of inflicting on herself.

At the end of her second year in high school she had experienced something similar and that categorically confirmed her decision. Her parents suddenly got after her to see her cousin, it was really strange, the two families were in vague contact at best, they got together a few times a year and she had no opinion about her cousin whatsoever. She let them convince her and called her on the phone. Chloë, that was her cousin's name, didn't sound particularly enthusiastic, this was clearly some idiotic parental conspiracy to bring their daughters together, but in the end why shouldn't they see each other, so they set up a time and Chloë brought her to a darkened café with a pool table that reeked of cigarette smoke. She offered her a cigarette, Sirma lit up, she had started smoking in elementary school, trying to be cool, but actually didn't like it at all and waited impatiently for her clique at the time to fall apart so she could quit smoking, but she'd mastered the mannerisms—with a cigarette in her hand she could pass for a dyed-in-the-wool smoker and that sometimes came in handy, she was more adaptable than Spartacus or Maya who had never smoked a cigarette in their lives and often earned themselves funny looks because of this. As it was the afternoon, the café was half-empty, they were all friends of Chloë and they looked as if they lived there. In the greenish light two boys were expertly playing pool and she was staring at the table, she liked the rhythmic clicking of the balls, her cousin was smoking silently and anxiously chewing the cigarette between her lips, Sirma looked her over carefully, she was heavily made up, her hair was bleached platinum and for the moment, despite her anxiousness, she seemed relieved not to have to walk, because she was wearing shoes with monstrously high heels that were clearly wrenching her ankles. Sirma had presciently left her army-surplus backpack and worn-out jean jacket at home, but she still sensed that she looked out of place there, her cousin had wrenched her feet from her shoes, they were clearly digging into her, her toenails were painted purple. Sirma had never gotten a pedicure. She and Spartacus and Maya made fun of the girls at school decked-out like poodles, who made fun of them in turn. She felt ridiculous. She had no reason for being there. The drinks were expensive, there was no one she could talk about music with, she was used to sitting on the grass in the park and though she still liked the rhythmic clicking of the billiard balls and the boys with their skillful, confident movements, she started feeling smothered. At the other end of the café, beyond the pool table, there was something like a raised upper level with a single solitary table, from which several older boys were contemplating them lazily. They were good-looking guys, and with their absent-minded expressions, with the apathetic superiority that radiated from their table, they seemed to lift it even higher, into some cloud-filled dimension from which they watched the mortals' games with the distant, languid interest of Olympians, or perhaps it only seemed that they were watching, when in fact their divine minds had wandered off somewhere else entirely, into the unseen and the unfathomable. The glass door of the café opened and another girl came in, with tight jeans and a leather jacket, she was pretty, with blonde hair and soft features, everybody livened up at her entrance, her cousin straightened up and puffed on her cigarette more energetically, one of the boys lazily slapped the newcomer on the ass as she walked by the pool table, and she made as if to kick him. The girl came over to them, Chloë pointed at Sirma, this is my cousin, but she didn't say her name or the name of her friend, the girl sized her up with a smile, but didn't say anything, she sat down by Chloë and they started a conversation that Sirma couldn't understand at all, they were talking about some guys with funny nicknames, about scag and A-bombs, about Nero and how an eighth kept him floating for three days, you know, and about some other guy who was probably a narc, so if Chloë saw him she should keep her distance. Then they started murmuring quietly and Sirma guessed they were talking about her, her cousin frowned when the new girl turned to her and asked her if she wanted a jay. Sirma gaped at her. A joint, man, you know. Aaah, why didn't you just say so, girl, she tried to get into their style. She had only smoked a joint once, Spartacus had scrounged it up somewhere, dug it up from the bottom of his backpack, hidden among the little plastic figurines and dead pens; and since unlike her friends, she had experience with cigarettes, she had managed to not cough while they smoked it, but nothing happened to her at all, nor to them, either. The girl in the leather jacket took out a joint and handed it to her cousin. You guys can have it, she said, my throat is killing me, I can't smoke right now. The others saw the joint and started milling around them. Are we gonna smoke it here, Sirma asked incredulously. Of course, her cousin replied, the bartender is down, so don't freak. She lit the joint and took a drag, the sweetish scent of weed wafted heavily in the air, they passed it around twice and it was gone. Sirma waited for that mellowing she'd heard about, but after a long time she still didn't feel anything and decided that she must not have smoked it right again. Her cousin, however, had mellowed out, it was as if the shared weed had lowered her guard a bit. Looks like Chopper's gone horse-riding, the girl in the leather jacket said and nodded towards the raised table at the other end of the café. Yeah, looks that way to me, too, her cousin replied, seeming impressed. They fell silent for a while. C'mon, let's go hunting, said the girl with the leather jacket. Her cousin took a deep drag off her cigarette. But now I'm feeling all peaceful and shit, she said, from the weed. Don't give me that, the other girl said. You need the money. True, Chloë said, but still, you know. She had her back to Sirma so she couldn't see what kind of gestures she was making to the other girl, but she figured that again they had to do with her. But her friend just kept smiling, completely calm. Chloë turned to her and looked at her carefully. Sirma, I can count on you, right? How about making some money, huh? Whatever you say, Sirma shrugged. *Whatever you say*, she mimicked her, and Sirma suddenly realized that her cousin was drunk, she had obviously been drinking before she met up with her, she was slurring her words and looking through her towards something, so much so that she herself was tempted to turn around to see just what was so interesting behind her back. C'mon, said the other girl, come with us and we'll show you how it's done.

They went outside and started walking quickly. It was already getting dark. Sirma hurried after them, annoyed, and wondered whether the weed hadn't gotten to her at least a little this time. They stopped two blocks later and turned down a side street, there was a school a bit farther up and the kids were walking home in little groups. One lone chubby girl with a big backpack passed by them, the girl with the leather jacket shot out and grabbed her by the shoulder. Hey, she said softly, gimme your money. What money, the girl with the backpack mumbled. Sirma was stunned. She, too, had gotten jumped on the street, they'd demanded her money, and she, too, had instinctively answered with the same stupid and pointless answer: *What money?* This kind, the girl with the leather jacket said and shoved her prey up against the wall. She brought her face close to the girl's and for an instant Sirma felt like she herself was up against the wall, she felt the other girl's aggressive breath scalding her lips, then suddenly things turned around and now she was the girl with the leather jacket pressing her victim's shoulders hard, she could do whatever she wanted to her, and in the next instant she came back to her real place, standing and watching, hypnotized by the sight, by the power and the aggression streaming from the girl in the leather jacket, she suddenly raised her knee and hit the fat girl in the stomach, she let out a little moan, then mumbled, c'mon, let me go, she was on the verge of tears, and Sirma suddenly hated her for that powerless sniveling, then her cousin went up to them and said softly, come on, give us the money and nothing will happen to you, come on, don't beat her up, she's a good girl and she'll give us some cash, isn't that right, and the girl finally reached into her pocket and thrust some rumpled bills in her hand, yeah, she really is a good girl, said her cousin's friend, the other girl looked on helplessly as Chloë went through her pockets looking for more money, but there clearly wasn't any more, look in her backpack, her friend ordered, Chloë rifled through the backpack nervously and hurriedly, there's no wallet, she reported, I don't have any more, that's it, groaned the fat girl, but the blonde girl with the leather jacket kept holding her and repeating "oh, what a good girl" and suddenly she kissed her on the lips and laughed loudly, then she roughly spun her around and launched her up the street with a slap on the ass, come on already, what are you waiting for, her cousin hissed and pulled her into the street, her hand was warm and wet, the girl with the leather jacket appeared calmly from around the corner, she was still laughing, three fivers, said Chloë and hesitated for a moment, before adding, exactly even, she turned towards Sirma and handed her one of the bills, Sirma stared at the dirty, rumpled piece of paper, come on, take it, Chloë insisted, you're in on it, too, right? her hand was shaking, whether from adrenaline or from fear that she had shown too much without knowing whether she could trust her, and Sirma realized that she had no choice, she reached out and took the bill, it was old, greasy from the hundreds, perhaps even thousands of fingers that had passed it around. Her cousin sighed. Keep mine, the girl with the leather jacket said, you need it more than I do. Are you sure, Chloë said, yeah, of course I'm sure. They went back to the café with the pool table and her cousin ordered three vodkas at the bar. Sirma drank hers in one gulp and earned a round of applause. She felt keyed-up, her skin was prickling. Do you do that a lot, she asked her cousin. Oh yeah, she said. You ought to see us at a club. You won't believe how that chick can fight, she nodded towards her friend. She really is a witch or something, lemme tell you. She ripped out half of some girl's hair. See, she pulled down the collar of her shirt and showed her red scratch marks. That's from the last time we went clubbing, we got in a fight. But if anybody asks, I tell people some dude scratched me. The only problem is that weed is counterproductive for fighting, it makes you all mellow and stuff. Just look how nice we were tonight. Sirma started scraping her nails on the table her empty vodka glass was sitting on. One of the guys from the pool table, the better-looking one, sat down at their table and started making out with the third girl, whose name they still hadn't bothered to tell her. All of a sudden she was sick of it all. I've got to go, she told her cousin. Really? Too bad, she replied. Call me some other time. Yeah, okay. Hey, Chloë was suddenly serious, what happened tonight stays between us, okay, we're on the same team now, right? Absolutely, what, do you think I'm a squealer? No, no, of course now, it's just that . . . Okay whatever, you get me, right? No worries. She got up and went towards the door. Even if she was a squealer, that greasy bill guaranteed her silence. She turned around and saw the other girl licking the guy's ear, their eyes met and she winked at her. Sirma didn't react. The boys at the raised table kept watching them indifferently, as if they didn't exist at all for them. She opened up the glass door and stepped out into the dark, she quickly set out for home, but no matter how fast she walked, it still seemed too slow, as if her legs were sinking in some sticky swamp of disgust and euphoria, and she again entered the scene with the girl backed up against the wall, sometimes she was in her skin, sometimes she turned into the other girl, the attacker, and afterwards she melted down into nothing more than the touching of lips, into that unfathomable yet enchanting kiss of violence, she tried to blame her dazedness on the weed or the vodka, but she knew that wasn't it at all, that physically she was totally sober, and that she was spellbound by what she had seen alone, now she was imagining her cousin and the girl with the leather jacket tearing out other girls' hair, raking their faces with their nails, and then flying at each other, swinging their fists like boys, falling on the ground and, as they were fighting, they would suddenly start kissing in the noisy half-darkness, checkered by multi-colored lights, then again and again she would go back to the scene near the school, sometimes playing one role, sometimes the other, and that kept going until she finally fell into a pitch-dark, dreamless sleep. The next morning she woke up early for school, went to the kitchen, got herself a bowl of cereal, poured milk over it, and while she was waiting for it to soak in, she went over to the window and looked outside, down below there was a run-down playground with a few surrealistic jungle gyms and a dilapidated horse-shaped spring rider, all of a sudden she heard the blonde girl's voice in her head saying clearly *Looks like Chopper's gone horse-riding* and she suddenly realized what it meant, her stomach clenched and her diaphragm jumped, she heaved over the table, over the bowl of cereal, but she didn't have anything to throw up, only a stream of bitter stomach acid trickled into her mouth, she spit it into the sink and turned on the water.

Her uncle and aunt had clearly realized, they had figured out what was going on far too late and had come up with the completely stupid idea of finding new friends for their daughter, all of a sudden they had remembered that, hey, she has a cousin, well, of course, why not have her hang out with her cousin, who goes to a good school? Bent over the kitchen sink, Sirma felt rage, she had no desire to save her cousin, now she needed to save herself, to dissolve herself in water like a tablet and to drink herself down, she now hated her cousin for cracking open that door, which should have stayed shut, she had shown her vileness, which she had in fact liked, as if someone were teaching her to eat her own shit. On the bunk of the ferryboat to Rhodes, Sirma was suddenly paralyzed by a deeply forgotten memory, from when she was a kid and had been playing with a little boy in the neighborhood park, their grandmas were sitting on the benches and not keeping much of an eye on them as they played and chased each other, Sirma suddenly caught a strong whiff of shit, she grabbed the little boy by the hand and told him he'd stepped in poo, he lifted his foot and looked at the sole of his shoe, it was smeared with a reeking yellow mess, now watch this, he said, sat down on the ground and with the natural flexibility of small children lifted his leg, brought the shoe towards his face and licked it. In the bunk, Sirma again sprang up in wave of nausea, just like that morning over the cereal, and just like then, she had nothing to throw up, only a stream of stomach acid stung her tongue. Back then, that morning over the kitchen sink, she had decided to reduce her world to Spartacus and Maya. Before going out, she quietly went back to her room, pulled the dirty, rumpled bill out of her pocket and stuffed it in the bottom of the cupboard where she had kept various important things ever since she was a kid, the fiver stayed there up until she moved away from home. When she was gathering up her stuff she found it, she had almost forgotten about it, and since a lot of time had passed since then, she gathered the strength to reach towards the cinnamon-scented candle she liked to light in the evenings and to burn it up.

But her cousin sank and miraculously surfaced again, and Sirma was thankful to her for the latter, because, even though the two families had never really been close, they surely would never have forgiven her desertion if Chloë had died of an overdose, as seemed to be the case with many of her friends. She simply got lucky. Her father, Sirma's uncle, found a job in Austria and they left; once cut off from the café with the pool table, where the barman was *down*, Chloë became a perfectly normal girl, she had already learned German and was studying some sort of economics. Sirma never did figure out how seriously her cousin had gotten *hooked* on heroin, but since the people around her were dying off, it clearly was no joke, and if that were the case, then she really had needed money, and that *shakedown* by the school was surely no isolated incident, she had done it regularly with the girl with the leather jacket, whose face Sirma could not recall for some reason, but she would remember her from time to time and would also remember that on that evening, she hadn't smoked the joint, she hadn't taken the money they had snatched from the scared girl on the street, she hadn't even sipped the vodka Chloë had bought with the money. After her uncle's family left for Austria, some long-forgotten kinship ties had suddenly reawakened, the fathers started writing emails and talking on the phone (Skype hadn't yet become a mass phenomenon) and one day, right around the time Elena had appeared in their midst and Sirma had met her with instinctive hostility, because she threatened the inviolability of their trinity, her father triumphantly announced that they were going to visit Vienna. Sirma had nothing against setting aside a week of her vacation for Vienna. But when the day came for them to leave, Elena had already launched her attack dizzyingly fast, she had jumped from Maya to Spartacus, she was drowning him in sex and in doing so seemed to have lost Maya, who understandably was sincerely jealous now, but she had driven a wedge between the two of them and Spartacus, and Sirma left for Vienna with the bad feeling that in her absence things would get even worse. Dance a Viennese waltz for us, Spartacus joked before she left, and at that moment everything was just as before, but she knew that in the evening he would meet Elena and she imagined his hands unzipping her jeans, his fingers sinking into the yielding pink flesh. Her cousin really had become a perfectly normal girl and Sirma was happy for her, she realized that until now she had always been ashamed of that evening and of the fact that she had never called Chloë again, despite her parents' urging. The two families strolled the streets and took photos of themselves in front of the extravagant, cream-pie buildings, Sirma had bought herself a new digital camera and one evening it occurred to her that she could show Chloë pictures of her friends, they hooked the camera up to the computer and she tried to explain to her, insofar as it was possible, her relationship with Spartacus and Maya, and Elena was in one of the pictures, too, Sirma groaned and explained that she was just some annoying chick who was trying to glom onto them, but her cousin abruptly fell silent, Sirma looked at her, she sat frozen, staring at the screen with unblinking eyes, hey, said Sirma, what's the matter, she did not take her eyes off the picture, that's Elena, she said finally. Yeah, Sirma said in surprise, her name is Elena, do you know her, of course I know her, Chloë said at last, don't you remember her? Some powerful wave hit her on the head and sent her back to that bizarre and repulsive evening, she heard Elena's voice, *oh, what a good girl* and felt her strange kiss on her own lips and only now could she reconstruct the image that had buried itself somewhere deep in the corners of her memory, the face of the girl with the leather jacket.

As she could conclude from that evening, Elena had never gotten hooked on drugs, nor had she needed the money she squeezed out of those frightened girls, sometimes with a kiss, and sometimes by bloodying their noses, she had more than enough money, she had done it for fun and when she had gone to the café with the pool table and all the other places people went to hang out and get high, that was also for fun, she knew everybody: Chopper, who had gone horse-riding; Nero, who had floated for three days on an eighth; and the guy who was probably a narc, now all three of them were dead, as well as lots of others, such as the two guys Sirma had seen playing pool so well. Chloë spoke softly and swallowed, her eyes dry, if she had ever felt the urge to cry for those people, she had clearly already cried everything out. Elena was like some apparition, a witch, she said, and Sirma remembered that she had used that word even then, but as a compliment, she had always been hanging around them but never with them, she had watched, laughed and enjoyed seeing them writhe in the sticky semi-darkness, sometimes she told them what scum they were, while the next time she'd tell them how much she loved them, and she often gave them money to buy junk, and then at one point she simply disappeared, vanished into thin air, she just got sick of it, Sirma thought, and changed groups, now she knew what had repulsed her about that girl from the first day Maya brought her around, she knew why she had felt uneasy in her presence, as if lightened and naked, and she knew that immediately upon her return that she had to chase her far away from Spartacus.

She suddenly wanted to see Spartacus leaning over the railing with a map in his hand, struggling to figure out exactly which island they were passing, but refusing to ask a crew member, Maya, too, with her camera, and Krustev, proud to be in the company of nice young people. Sirma wriggled out of the bunk, left the cabin and set off into the labyrinth of corridors and narrow, steep staircases. She wandered for quite a while before finding the others amid the multi-colored, multi-lingual crowds on the deck, it was five in the afternoon and they were already far south, the sun was noticeably sinking towards the sea, but as it sank, it grew ever larger and continued beating down, right on the nape of the neck. Hey, Spartacus turned to her when she finally found them, we're already getting close, you missed some amazing views, but soon we should be able to see Rhodes, aren't you excited to see your great-grandfather's island? When they had decided to go to Rhodes, Sirma had called home and asked for precise information about the family's mythical Lydian roots, her father had explained to her that the story really was downright mythical, his grandfather had been a Lydian from Rhodes and family legend had it that he had run away from home as a boy after his drunk father threatened to kill him and boil him up for stew. Her great-grandfather became a cabin boy on a ship and since, of course, this was back in Macedonian times, he had sailed the empire's five seas, until he finally decided to settle down somewhere whence he'd have to travel three days on a donkey to catch the scent of the sea, and thus he arrived in the sleepy Thracian village, where, as a result of this strange great-grandfatherly whim, Sirma's grandfather had been born. Unlike her father, Sirma had never been interested in their family history. She remembered a yellowed photograph of her great-grandfather— who in the world had travelled three days by donkey in order to photograph him in that mountain village?—but in any case, the picture had captured an angry old man with a huge white mustache and something like a turban, she was really surprised by the turban and suspected that her great-grandfather had been a Muslim, but her father explained that at that time Christians had also worn turbans on Rhodes and the nearby islands. There were yet more mysteries surrounding the great-grandfather from Rhodes: participation in an uprising, a wound to the shoulder, some hazy irregularities in how he came by a wife. But now thanks to chance they were going to the very island where her great-grandfather was almost boiled into stew by his own father and Sirma couldn't deny that her curiosity was growing; what do you know about Rhodes and about Lydia, she asked Spartacus, thanks to his job at the tourist agency he had become a reliable source of easily digestible information about the region, well, the Colossus, Spartacus said. Even I know about the Colossus, Sirma said, it stood at the entrance to the harbor and ships would pass between its legs, a huge statue, one of the seven wonders of the world, right, can you list all of them? I can, replied Spartacus, but only one other one was located in present-day Lydia, namely the Temple of Artemis at Ephesus, and he looked at her triumphantly, besides, he added, it isn't true at all that the Colossus was straddling the harbor and that ships passed between its legs, that's more legend than anything else, too bad it only stood for sixty years or so, an earthquake destroyed it. That is too bad, Sirma said, surely the wrath of the gods caused the earthquake, they didn't like people building such a huge statue, like the Tower of Babylon, the gods don't like hubris, Spartacus agreed. What don't they like? According to Spartacus, hubris was when you are really haughty and arrogant, and in order to act like a big shot you transgress against the divine order of things, but to her it sounded like the name of a rare herb that was part of the recipe for chai. The Lydian king Croesus is also an example of hubris, Spartacus noted. Wasn't Croesus the one who was really rich? In Spartacus's story, Croesus, besides being filthy rich and possibly being the first to hit upon the idea of minting money, went to war against the Persians, but not before asking the Oracle of Delphi for advice and the oracle predicted that if he went to war, he would destroy a great empire, Croesus was overjoyed and rushed into battle, and only when he had suffered utter defeat did he realize that he truly had destroyed a great empire, namely his own, but while he was fretting and fuming, the Persians caught him and their King Cyrus, whom the Jews otherwise considered very cool and tolerant, since he had allowed them to return to their homeland from Babylonian exile, ordered that he be burned at the stake. So they tied Croesus to the stake, lit it and everything was going as planned, Cyrus was looking on and enjoying himself, however right when the flames were about to reach him, Croesus cried out despairingly: "Solon! Solon! Solon!" Cyrus was intrigued as to the meaning of this cry and since his translators could only tell him that Solon was a famous Athenian wise man, he ordered them to put out the fire and bring Croesus to him. It turned out that some time earlier, Croesus and the wise man Solon had argued about human happiness and Croesus had claimed that he was the happiest person in the world, since he had everything: a strong empire, enormous wealth, a beautiful wife, wonderful children; but Solon told him that there were at least two men who had been happier than Croesus and they were twin brothers who had died in their sleep because their mother had begged the goddess Hera to give them the greatest possible happiness. So it turns out that happiness is a peaceful death, Maya broke in, who, along with Krustev, had been listening to the lecture carefully. That's how it turns out, Spartacus agreed, but Sirma bit her lips, because it probably wasn't a very good idea to philosophize about death in front of Krustev, who had obviously lost his wife recently and didn't want to talk about it; in any case, Spartacus continued, Croesus had already lost his son, who had been killed accidentally by a friend of his, his wife had committed suicide out of grief and now there he was, the former ruler of a collapsed empire, about to be roasted at the stake by foreigners, however, Cyrus was put to shame by the story, just as Croesus had been right before the flames engulfed him, and since the two of them were so ashamed, Cyrus decided he would do well to spare Croesus's life and hired him as an advisor. So, Spartacus concluded, Croesus showed hubris by claiming to be the happiest man on earth; and fate, with its innate love of irony, decided to show him that this wasn't quite the case; but, in fact, hubris is indivisibly coupled with shame, because with pride and arrogance you not only demean others, but in the end you shame yourself, while on the other hand it was precisely shame that saved Croesus, right, there aren't many people like him, who could say that they saved their own lives thanks to the fact that they suddenly and at exactly the right time were ashamed of what stupid bastards they had been up to that point. What's more, at least according to Ancient Greek mythology, it turns out that Lydia is definitely the land of hubris and hence of shame, for example, the story of Niobe, who boasted that she was better than Artemis's mother because she had more children and was more beautiful, is quite similar, Artemis and Apollo went and slaughtered all of her children as punishment; except that the story about Croesus could easily be true, I think it comes from Herodotus. You are Herodotus, Sirma said, but she didn't tell them about her great-grandfather, who had sailed the five seas and afterwards settled in a remote mountain village three days' journey by donkey from the scent of the sea, the angry great-grandfather with the moustache twisted up like hubris.

[9]

Krustev felt a little duped because instead of watching the boat arrive, instead of seeing the island dust off its dress uniform to meet the new arrivals, he had to go down to the car and get ready to leave. But he left the kids up on deck to watch the palace of the Grand Master rise above the dappled coast, stern and supercilious, and at least that was some consolation, as if some part of him would stay there, too, watching. Without noticing it and without meaning to, he had already slipped into their net of key words and tacit agreements, and he was forced to admit that this made him feel good. When he stopped on that Rhodope road and picked them up, he had simply wanted company, people to chat with, to distract him, and to have some immediate goal, in order to drive them to it. But from then on everything had developed so quickly and simply, and the mutual discomfort they had felt, he with them and they with him, was actually more helpful than not, for example on the beach on Thasos he had tried to look aside so as not to stare at Sirma's brazenly displayed breasts, this had, in fact, brought him closer to them, some quiet thread of shame gleamed in the sunlight for an instant, weaving yet another tie between them. Alone in his car, in the garage, winded from the gas fumes, Krustev told himself that whatever the three teenagers' secret was, he didn't want to know it, he wasn't enticed by the possibility of muscling his way between them, of digging through the strange space enclosed by their triangle, and he was thankful that they returned the gesture, not asking him why he had taken off on his own and what had happened, and if they had guessed, they didn't pursue their conjectures with the doggedness of a blind hunter, something he remembered so well from his own youth, back then he had probed every patch of earth, digging down to reach a spring, and once he had drunk from the precious water, he lost interest, just as when he had played his solo and had to return to the familiar and steady rhythm of the song and somehow hold out until the end of it.

Rhodes didn't seem to have changed since he had been there with Irina and Elena; while driving along the narrow, cobblestone streets of the old town, once again astonished that they were open to cars, Krustev tried to remember when exactly it had been, maybe seven years ago, or eight, yes, because Elena had certainly been, say, twelve, a girl, in whose body a woman's figure was hesitantly emerging and this woman who was furtively sneaking into her confused her reactions, imperceptibly casting her shadows, doing with his daughter as she wished. If it had been possible to be jealous of his daughter's relationship with her own self, perhaps that was what he had felt during that vacation, especially one day on the beach, when he emerged from the sea, heading towards their umbrella and she didn't look at him at all, she had turned her head the other direction, and he turned, following her gaze, and his eyes collided with the muscular body of the lifeguard, and this staggered him more than if he had caught his own wife ogling the lifeguard with the little gold cross on his chest, and that was also the first vacation when he didn't feel like sleeping with Irina, even though they had rented a suite at the hotel and Elena slept in a separate room, they simply fell asleep every night and neither one of them was particularly struck by this lack of desire, there was something here to fill the gaping empty space with, ice cream and cocktails, and walks through the old town, and coarse brown sand, as if for construction, you could fill bags with sand and easily soar through the air knowing you had something to unload if you started plunging downward.

They found a room at the end of the old city, on one of those streets that was so narrow that even pedestrians, especially the tubbier ones, could hardly pass, and at a reasonably good price so that the three of them were not taken aback by the size of the gift being given them; after they brought their luggage inside, Sirma went outside with Krustev and stood in front of the entrance, her mouth gaping open, looking at the crooked outline of the house, the flaking green façade and the window frames warped by the salty moisture, wow, she said, my whole life I've dreamed of living in a place like this, and Krustev smiled, the four-person room was narrow and dark, the windows actually looked out onto the wall across the way, but he understood Sirma very well, it was so *interesting* to live in such a house, for a few days, of course, and he was glad that he had overcome his own habit of comfort in order to go up the creaking stairs ducking his head and to breathe in the scent of old wood and the mossy stone wall, there was something very *real* about this house and the others like it nearby, a scrap of real life amid the whole touristic bacchanalia with its flip-flops, brand-name handbags and ridiculous souvenirs, there was life, which created the illusion that it was more real than your own, but still Krustev did not give himself over completely to sentimental ecstasy and carefully checked the bathroom and the water heater before paying. He left the car in a parking lot beyond the fortress walls, they wouldn't need it inside, the three of them could hardly stay in one place, they wanted to wander everywhere, peek into every passageway, to touch every stone, he smiled in satisfaction and from time to time wondered why the hell he couldn't go somewhere with his daughter in the same way, what were these barriers that arose between you and those closest to you, making impossible the things you were free to do with people you met by chance along the way, and in that case how had these three toppled all the barriers between them, or perhaps the more precise question was how had they prevented the barriers from arising? He looked at them and couldn't imagine them separately, even though now Maya, now Sirma, now Spartacus hung back from the others and walked with him to talk, in the beginning on Thasos he had felt a certain forcedness in how suddenly one of the three of them would remember his presence and sheepishly come keep him company, now that feeling was gone, and at times he could even tell himself that he wasn't twenty-odd years older than them, for example, when they were teaching him to swim with laughter and enthusiasm, encouraging him and he was catching on quickly, he could already keep himself floating on the surface and now the most important part was to coordinate his arms and legs, he thought that would be easy, he was a musician after all, with a sense of rhythm and timing, but he still hadn't quite managed it.

That night he couldn't fall asleep for a long time, listening to their steady breathing, truth be told the bed was too narrow and the mattress sagged, plus his dinner wasn't sitting well in his stomach, he suddenly realized that he had chalked up his sleeplessness precisely to these everyday causes, while only a few days earlier he would have known that the reason was actually something else and he would have gone out to look at the birch trees, white as hospital walls; lying on the sagging mattress, he asked himself whether he should feel guilty that he was a few thousand miles from home in the pleasant company of young people, having thrown off his grief and depression like flannel pajamas, but wasn't that why he'd set off aimlessly in his car, to slip away, at the time he hadn't known either where he was going, or when he would come back, because he wasn't thinking of returning, he just needed to go somewhere else, to go far away, and now it was ridiculous to feel guilty in front of his dead wife, she certainly would have approved. Krustev sighed and thought about how Irina had always been smarter than him, even in her death she remained smarter, surely some change was taking place within him now which he didn't quite fully understand, but she would've figured out, just as she had figured out before him that their marriage had gone cold and she had accepted it with that strange calm with which she took in everything, even in the wild years when they had met. He was always a step behind her, and eight years ago was no exception

either, when they had come here to Rhodes and had not made love
even once, yet he had desired another woman, he remembered
her all of a sudden, blonde and slippery, sitting at the hotel bar,
Irina and Elena were out shopping, he had gone to have a drink,
they started talking, she was from Belgium or Holland, what is an
attractive woman like you doing here all alone, God, how stupid
and banal, it's like stepping in something sticky in the fallen leaves
and saying to yourself god damn it I just stepped in shit, but it
turns out that it's only soft mud, he wanted her lazily, with the
superiority of a successful man, and after all that's why she was sitting alone at the bar, and while she spoke to him slowly, purring,
he imagined taking her to his suite and tossing her down on the
double bed or better yet, on his daughter's bed, why not, screwing
this easy woman on his daughter's bed, and amid the astringent
taste of this vision he suddenly felt ashamed, not from any sense
of fidelity, not because he had decided that it was disgusting, but
because it was not disgusting *enough* and that made it ridiculous,
he hadn't stepped in shit, but in mud, and every day men and
women like the two of them sat at that bar, and they would continue sitting there until the hotel got old and was torn down, and
after a new one was built in its place, those men and women with
their repulsive smiles and worn-out lines would continue sitting
there, and he started backing off, she sensed it, turned away, his
phone rang, it was his partner from the promotional agency, who
ecstatically roared in his ear dude, we got Rammstein, that was
amazing news, they had been fighting Thracian Entertainment for
that concert, they had turned somersaults to get this deal, and now
they were becoming a leading player in the industry and Krustev
barked into the phone *wunderbar!*

But, as he had come to realize years later, around the time they had won the Rammstein gig, his wife had already started seeing her director, he never did find out where she'd met him, whether he was blond or dark, whether he did Shakespeare or Pinter; she simply mentioned him once, when it was already completely clear to both of them that their relationship was more that of roommates, otherwise polite and considerate of each other, she mentioned to him that for five years she'd had a boyfriend who was a director, a theater director, she said, as if saying in passing that last night she'd been to a restaurant with her girlfriends, an Italian restaurant, and Krustev was stunned by his lack of jealousy, well okay, he replied, but I don't want to see him, Irina agreed, afterwards he felt hurt, even though he knew he had no such right, he himself also had mistresses, and not just one or two, and perhaps that was precisely what changed things, he had scattered his sexual instinct, which was in any case blunted by work, among many women, while Irina had simply replaced him with another, she had found herself another man and she surely even loved him, it was just that she didn't live with him, but no one mentioned divorce, the wounded Krustev's first thought was that his wife, of course, did not want to deprive herself of the house, the car and everything else, of her secure and comfortable life, and that very well may have been part of it, but besides that she was surely afraid that if she got divorced and started living with her director, sooner or later their relationship would wither just like her marriage had. Does Elena know, he asked her, I've only hinted about it to her, Irina replied, Krustev suddenly wondered whether he would be expected to move out of the nuptial bed, but in fact, this foreign object, his wife's body, did not bother him and she did not leave the bed, either, presumably the force of habit was too powerful, and with such an obvious act of separation, they would have had to give their daughter definite explanations. This conversation had taken place only three years earlier, so that means, Krustev calculated, that Elena had been seventeen then and sufficiently tuned in to sense what was going on even without her mother's hinting. At that time, Krustev sometimes stared at his daughter in astonishment, momentarily stunned by the memory of that erstwhile baby in his arms and unable to understand what the pretty young girl in his living room could possibly have in common with that surprised little tuft of life, two so very different creatures, who by some coincidence bore the same name. Elena seemed to be going through some teenage crisis, from which she recovered on her own and he made sure not to grill her too much, he felt ill at ease rummaging around in his daughter's life with his rough, manly paws and he certainly wouldn't have understood anything of her problems and worries, the parade of pimply boyish faces, the staggering, terrible meaning that even the most casual words take on at that age, maybe six months before that, yes, that's about how long it had been, he had started becoming seriously worried about Elena, she was out and about far more than she should be, she would silently lock herself away in her room, and when she would come out or come home, she looked steel-plated in her leather jacket, scornful and—in some vague and disturbing way—evil. What more could she want, he would sometimes ask himself the question of all parents from all continents and eras, and when he would catch himself thinking such thoughts, he would sullenly decide that he was starting to get old, not physically, but in his perceptions, in the automatic schemata through which one thinks about the world, and he would even tell himself that if he hadn't become a father and husband so early, he would surely feel younger right now, he wasn't even forty. But right when Irina had casually mentioned her theater director, her tagliatelle with gorgonzola, he had stopped worrying about his daughter, because she looked a lot better, she was sociable, as the doctors loved to put it, the two of them would talk, and nothing seemed strange or wrong to him, and besides, back when she was still out and about, she had never come home drunk and Krustev simply could not believe that was possible. And still listening to the three young people's steady breathing, lying in the dark on the uncomfortable mattress, he wondered which Elena they knew, what had happened between them and whether he wanted to know or not. It was him, not Elena who was doing something wrong, chumming up with her friends, albeit her former friends, secretly, through the back door, he was sneaking into her personal life, so carefully hidden from her parents, just as it should be, and having once ended up inside this forbidden house accidentally and in the absence of its master, perhaps it would nevertheless be best not to act like a bull in a china shop, not to break or rearrange things, not to leave muddy footprints on the floor and not even to look around, but simply to sit with his eyes closed, until the time came to leave. He sighed. He had lost both his wife and his daughter, and if the loss of the former was in large part his own fault, the loss of the latter could not be helped, it was the natural result of the mechanical march of time, from a certain point onward our own children belong to us less than any other person around. He suddenly felt like sitting down with Elena again, like they had during the winter, when with her soccer banter she had unexpectedly wrenched him from his stupor, he wanted to bring out the bottle of scotch with two glasses and say with his unused voice, so now tell me what's going on with you, back then she had told him some things, hinted at others, it seemed that leaving for the States had been very important to her, not just because of the university and the opportunities, but because it allowed her to break away from something or someone here, where her life had passed until then, and now her mother, her mother's body tied up in its tubes, had called her back at the beginning of beginnings, Elena didn't want to stay here. So he had assured her that he would be all right and sent her off to America, after which he proceeded to read all the books in the house and lose sleep. He knew he should be very grateful to her. In fact, she really didn't know anything about soccer. She had read a pile of articles about the upcoming match and had learned the players' names from pictures on the Internet, just to be able to talk to him.

He imperceptibly dropped off to sleep during the night and woke up only when the human presence leaning over his face pulled him out of the depths into which he had sunk. It was Maya, she was looking down on him with a slyly bashful smile, uh, it's eleven o'clock already, she said, we were thinking of going to check out the beach, the water here must be a lot warmer than on Thasos. They had to walk quite a ways before finding an open space with fewer tourists, the season had already begun and the hordes crawled in tireless ranks between the hotels and the beach. The shoreline was covered with tiny pebbles and Maya grumbled that she would cut her feet, which wasn't far from the truth, and after hesitantly wobbling around at the water's edge for a while, Spartacus dashed forward, scooped her up despite her protests, carried her out to sea and simply tossed her in the water, you'll drown me, you idiot, she screamed, well, he giggled, I've been meaning to for a while, and now I finally got my chance. Sirma was standing a little aside, up to her neck in water and watching them indulgently, momentarily amused by their childish antics. Krustev tried floating on his back, at first he thought he'd done it, but then it suddenly turned out that he was lying diagonally in the water with his feet almost touching the bottom. The sea was choppy, the tightly packed waves approached from the horizon and rocked their unmoored bodies, today isn't so great for swimming lessons, Sirma said, still, the water is a lot warmer than on Thasos, that goes without saying, Maya swam up to them panting, her face red from her battle with Spartacus. It's nice, said Krustev.

They ate gyros downtown, that was good, Maya said, but now I can just tell that I reek like garlic, come on now, Krustev joked, we're not gonna kiss each other, right, and suddenly he realized that it sounded exactly as if Spartacus had said it and the three of them didn't react, the comment sailed past just as their own routine comments did, springing up so naturally amid their conversations that they didn't even find them funny anymore, and he felt his chair rising slightly off the ground and swaying in the air, that same sense of rocking and the loss of solid ground that he felt in the sea. He took them through the old town's narrow, fantastic streets, lorded over by haughty, regal cats in the lazy afternoon, and that became yet another easily lost day, for months now all his days had been lost, but until now he had been at pains to lose them, he had wriggled through the cramped holes in the rough, scraping walls with effort; here, where the streets really were cramped and the walls rough, he couldn't sense the sand draining away; but when evening came and the city again filled up with tourists eager to buy sandals and silver bracelets, to eat heavy, impressive dishes and to drink bad wine, Krustev already knew where he wanted to go, and he knew that he wanted to go alone. They had set out to walk around the old town along the fortress wall, this was actually his idea, but he had forgotten that it was quite a hike, at one point Sirma announced that she'd had enough, you guys go on ahead, and sat down on the grass along the path, come on, lazybones, Spartacus goaded her indignantly, but she was already leaning against a crooked tree and taking off her sandals. Spartacus waved dismissively and he and Maya continued on, I'll stay here with her, Krustev called after them and sat down in the grass across from the girl who was intently massaging her toes, and felt the urge to light up a cigarette, a long abandoned habit, which from time to time cut through his consciousness like a flashback, the consolation of having something in your hand, the awkwardness of just sitting there doing nothing. How is she, Sirma asked him suddenly, how is Elena, and only now did he stop to think that she alone of the three hadn't said a word about his daughter until now, I think she's fine in the States, he said cautiously, not because he was hesitating as to what to say, but because he didn't know whether what he was saying was true, and plucked a blade of grass, started chewing on it and admitted, I don't really know her at all. Sirma seemed about to say something, but then kept quiet. Now was his chance to slip away for a few hours, he tried to explain and she seemed to understand immediately, you must've been here with Elena and your wife, and she nodded at his left hand, and Krustev said, yeah, I was with them, now he already knew that they knew, and Sirma knew that he knew that they knew, but she didn't ask anything more, silence about silence, Krustev said to himself, I don't ask them about their stuff and they don't ask me about my wife's death, what on earth could I tell them, that my wife went to the seaside with her boyfriend, whom she'd been with for eight years, someone I may have read about in the papers, but I didn't want to know who he was and now I'll certainly never find out, they had gone to the seaside together, she could swim, unlike me, but she got caught in the undertow and when they pulled her out of the water, she wasn't dead, but she wasn't alive either, and it was only then, when I went to see her in that white room that I could again speak honestly and openly with her, and yes, as you guessed, she died, and it's a bit of a long story, but in the end I grabbed my car keys and credit cards, left the house and hit the road, yes. Go, said Sirma, go, you don't need to explain, everybody needs time alone, remember that Guns N' Roses song, *everybody needs somebody, you're not the only one*, but sometimes you need to be *the only one*, right? What, you don't think that we always keep tabs on one another, go on, and if you're late getting back, we'll meet up at the apartment, but if not—you've got our phone numbers.

He found the place more by feel than by memory, he had gone there only one single time eight years ago, a stupid tourist with his wife and daughter, but he had been told to definitely visit that humble and inconspicuous little restaurant far from the tourist joints, where it showed that locals also lived on Rhodes, here you didn't order food, the owner decided for you and brought it over himself, an elderly, bony Lydian with a white beard and a huge moustache, with blue eyes and a salty face, as if he had just stepped off the fishing boat, he served his guests with respect and spry gestures, in which there was not a trace of the sycophantic servility demonstrated by the waiters in the usual restaurants, he moved briskly through the small space, carrying bowls of salads, plates of octopus, calamari, and mussels, which his wife prepared in the tiny kitchen behind the bar. Even Elena, who was known for reluctantly pushing food around her plate for half an hour, was impressed, now these were unpretentious, yet disconcertingly delicious appetizers, which they washed down with a liter of white wine and despite the stern glance from her mother, he poured some for Elena, too, for the first time he poured wine for her at the table, she took a sip cautiously, yet proudly, wrinkled up her nose and said it was a little sour, but otherwise all right, and drank her first glass of white wine along with the strange black dish which swallowed up the light, squid served in a sauce made of its own ink, if you were a writer, Elena said suddenly with one of her last fanciful, childlike whims, if you were a writer, you'd have to eat only this, an animal cooked in its own ink, being a writer, you'd have to eat ink, what do you say? They said that's exactly right and even shared this idea with the owner, he found it amusing and twisted his long moustache in satisfaction, well maybe your daughter will become a writer some day, if she eats ink regularly. Then Krustev turned his attention to the squid itself, incidentally, if you're a photographer it also made sense to eat it, but Elena's idea had lodged in his memory, because he thought of it from time to time, imagining a writer who ate ink sitting alone at the table, lost in thought and slightly scowling, dipping his bread in the black sauce and stuffing it into his mouth, now after all those books he had read over the winter, in which the people and the stories from the printed page seemed more real to him than everything around him and certainly more real than he himself was, he again wanted to eat squid ink, the strange, slightly tart taste of the sea and of something which cannot be defined, and for one more evening to draw close to the life of the man with the blue eyes and salty face and his heavy wife, who chopped, minced, fried and steamed, the two of them truly like something out of a book; and for that reason he had to go alone.

He found it; and it was the same, nothing about the place had changed, the same simple tables, the guitar hanging on the wall, and on the other wall—black-and-white photographs of old men from the islands, rugged, eternal old men, but among them there was one with huge, magnetic eyes, which seemed to have gathered all the possible dreams of his island, emanating them in his radiant gaze, which gushed from the picture and spilled throughout the space and far beyond it. The proprietor's beard was also as white, his moustache was also as long, Krustev sat down at one of the small tables, across from him four men were drinking ouzo, it was unusual for someone to come here alone, but he and the blue-eyed owner agreed on salad, squid and wine, he spoke English well, Krustev remembered that back then, too, they had been surprised that such an elderly man did so well with English, but perhaps he wasn't really as old as he looked, or perhaps he was eternal, like the old men in the photos. Krustev turned his eyes to the pictures and gave himself over to the oncoming return, the reversal of time, he let it pull him back into the sea, he once again thought of his grandfather, hidden behind a mask of rugged and scowling silence in the last house in the village, heavily treading the earth with his feet, how would he have gotten along with this spry man of the sea here, and right then he appeared with the plates and pulled him back into the present. Krustev broke off a chunk of bread, dipped it in the black squid sauce and involuntarily blurted out, I was here years ago, and back then my daughter said that this was a dish for writers . . . Because writers should eat ink, the owner added, well, yes, I remember all three of you, I was just wondering where I knew you from, years may have passed, but it's all stored up here and he tapped his forehead, I've got a memory like an elephant, I don't forget anything, and even if I want to, I can't, which is sometimes not a good thing at all, but other times is good, so did your daughter become a writer? I don't know, Krustev said foolishly. And he thought to himself that whatever he might be asked about his daughter, about his wife, he would be forced to reply *I don't know* far too often, he bit his lips and suddenly started talking, as if the chunk of bread soaked in ink had freed the long stopped-up stream, the swarms of words stuck in his body now poured out uninhibited in a language that was foreign to both of them; when he started telling him about his wife, the proprietor's salty face grew serious, until that moment he had been standing over the table, stunned, but now he pulled up a chair and looked at him carefully with his blue eyes and only when Krustev fell silent, winded, after he had told him about his daughter as well, and about the three young people and how he had brought them to Rhodes and about that self of his that he remembered from years ago, the raging Slav with the guitar from Euphoria, he told himself that he didn't know anyone else who was able to listen like that, you did right, the man said suddenly, sitting there across from him and looking at him with his blue eyes, and repeated you did right. Krustev felt himself blushing, he turned his eyes away and his gaze fell on the guitar. How long has it been since you've played, asked the old man. I don't know, Krustev smiled and realized that he didn't even know his name. Ardis, said the proprietor. Boril, Krustev replied and again wondered at the hard, marble sound of his given name. The squid had gone cold. And it shows that you loved to play when you were young, Ardis said. They called him from the other table, but he waved them off angrily and fixed his blue eyes on Krustev. Your daughter, I remember her very well, saying that about the ink, she was a smart girl, find her again. But first, eat up.

Krustev obediently finished off the cold squid and the salad, and drank the wine, only then did Ardis again grace him with his attention, he brought a bottle with two glasses the size of thimbles and sat down across from him, smiling. This is called *mastika*, he explained, they make it on the island of Chios and only there, from the sap of some special trees, they only have them on Chios. Now that you've eaten ink from the sea, he winked, some sap from the tree will do you good. Krustev wasn't sure if he should look for some hidden meaning in his words, because the old man clearly loved speaking in parables. But the sudden sweet scent of the drink hit his nostrils, refreshing him. Ardis, he said, the whole time, when I'm with these kids, I get the feeling that I should be ashamed. Well, of course, you're ashamed, replied the proprietor. If you weren't ashamed, I would have kicked you out of here long ago. Ardis got up abruptly, took the guitar off the wall and gave it to Krustev, he took it and carefully tried the strings and heard a voice that had sunk deeply in the sea of his own past, when Ardis told him take it, do you hear me, he said, take the guitar, I'm giving it to you.

[10] Since they had come to this island, everything had been somehow strange and unreal, as if the dreams she had dreamed recently had gradually escaped their designated boundaries and were at first hesitantly, then ever more freely and confidently having their way with reality. And perhaps it was also due to the approaching mysteries, they were supposed to be tomorrow, they would have to look for a secluded place tomorrow night and play out the ritual of their intimacy, theatrics which she had made up without much hope that the others would go along with it, but now look, it had been two years and they had done it every month

since Elena had left them, up until this week, when they had come across her father and he simply set off with them, he was an odd person, strange like his daughter and Sirma wasn't surprised when, hemming and hawing, he had begun explaining that he had to go somewhere on his own, besides it also immediately crossed her mind that tomorrow they would have to tell him the same thing, and now look, this was a golden opportunity that freed them from the need for unnecessary explanations or to sneak out during the night. The tree was digging into her back, but she stubbornly leaned against the twisted trunk, all around dusk was brushing the ground like a light blanket and in the warm twilight things took on an unreal appearance, the fortress wall, the bridge a little further on, and the bushes along the path, an empty bottle was lying slightly off to one side and in the falling dusk Sirma jumped in surprise upon seeing that it was a bottle of Thracian vodka, Terres, and she spent a long time staring foolishly at the bottle, Terres, that was the same vodka she had brought to Elena back then, she had taken a bottle of it to the office her father didn't use, she had slipped Spartacus's phone out of his pocket unnoticed the previous evening, while he, with his usual enthusiasm, had been talking about Radiohead's latest album and whining that they still hadn't come to Thrace, and by the way, now there's a good idea for Krustev and his promotional agency, but she hadn't gone to talk about that with his daughter: when she had called her on the phone, she wasn't even surprised, could she possibly have been expecting such an invitation to meet, that decisive clash, and she took advantage of her right to hold it on her own territory, you know, just to talk, Sirma had told her, and had gone over there with vodka, she didn't even know why she'd taken it, she wasn't hoping to get her drunk, she wasn't hoping to get drunk herself, but in fact, maybe they really had gotten drunk, she remembered that she left the bottle there half-empty, but a lot of time had passed, half-empty, just like Elena's story. You've come to get rid of me, Elena said directly, after she had poured them each a drink and they had sat down on the floor, facing each other, blue eyes against green, Elena in a tight green shirt and no bra, her round breasts clearly outlined, wearing close-fitting jeans, and she'd tossed her leather jacket onto the couch, and Sirma thought to herself that maybe she actually remembered her, that she had remembered her the whole time and had been playing with her, just as she played with Maya and Spartacus, and with all the others, you've come to get rid of me, Elena said, and Sirma replied yes, and the blood rushed into her ears when she repeated yes.

Until then she had never had a conversation like this with anyone. Elena told her everything, about her family, about the money and the house, the beautifully painted façade of their affluent life, about her school and how she had met Chloë, things that Sirma didn't want to know, didn't want to hear, but clearly that was the price she had to pay, so it was necessary to hear her out, was that it, would the witch finally shove off once she had blurted out everything, all the trash she had collected inside of her, or perhaps she expected Sirma to start feeling sorry for her, to hug her in consolation, to take her tear upon her cheek in an act of self-sacrifice and then patiently to offer up her other cheek, but the more she listened, the more she was unable to pity her, and the more she learned about her, the more difficult it was to understand her. It was so simple at first: there was this obnoxious tagalong, this schemer, who was trying to muscle her way into their triple life, but then she could also connect her with that green-eyed witch from years ago, the girl who squeezed money out of other girls with her fists and kisses and gave it to her friends to buy drugs, a girl who was simply evil and who loved watching others suffer; but now she was forced to find out more and more things about her life, to look at her face-to-face, a human being like all others, and to understand less and less her passion for meddling in the lives of others, for experimenting with them and watching them fall, as if projecting onto others some part of herself that she wanted to calmly examine and analyze from the outside. Elena's story jumped back and forth in time and in the end she stopped somewhere in her distant, half-forgotten childhood, when I got lost, Elena said, I only remember sitting on some gray street and watching some boys fight, it was amazing. An hour ago, two hours ago, before however much time had passed, Sirma would have been able to mock her, to make her look ridiculous, to tell her you're scum and stay the hell away from my friends, you're trapped, I'll simply tell them what I know, Spartacus isn't in love with you, it's just teenage hormones and you know it, and Maya is pissed at you, because she's jealous, plus for her the story of what happened that night would be more than enough, I'll tell them your story and there's nothing you can do about it. But now that story had swelled, it had become so bloated and heavy that it could no longer be told, not by someone else, and suddenly Sirma felt duped. It had become impossible to treat her like the scum that she was after those hours on the floor, blue eyes against green, she had walked right into her trap. What do you want, she asked, and Elena replied: Nothing. She fell silent and then repeated, I don't want anything, that's the problem. Well, Sirma said, despite the fact that she'd lost her nerve and was afraid that this was terribly obvious, well, I want you to leave us alone. Lucky you, Elena said, you know what you want, and she started laughing, she started laughing so resoundingly that Sirma felt humiliated, took a sip of her vodka, and said, well if you ask me, I think you want me to give you a nice big black eye. But Elena kept laughing and Sirma didn't hit her in any case, should she have hit her or not, that was the question, which even now she hadn't found an answer to, would she have defeated her if she'd hit her, or would she have been defeated, she didn't know, because, even though Elena really had left them alone, to this day she wasn't sure which of the two of them had won back then and this uncertainty was even more sickening than defeat; Elena, even from far off in time and space, possessed the ability to make everyone feel like a fool. You don't mind, do you, she said and reached for Sirma's glass, she had finished her own, and took a sip right from the place where Sirma's mouth had been, and gave her the glass back, she stared at the bright lipstick stain Elena had left, her lips on the glass, and suddenly she went back to that evening on the street, and once again she was jumping between the two bodies, that of the helpless girl up against the wall, and Elena's compact, aggressive body, and she was clearly drunk because even to this day she wasn't completely sure whether that moment had really happened or if it was just her imagination, had Elena really darted forward and kissed her on the lips, the same kiss which she had wrongfully and secretly felt that night, since it hadn't been meant for her, or perhaps it had, perhaps it had been meant precisely for her, for her alone, now she felt it again, but she didn't know whether it had happened in reality, in that which she could at least from time to time with a certain approximation call reality, because in the next instant Elena had returned to her place and was sitting there calm as can be, and all of that remained in a moment which had leapt into her time from some other, parallel time of passed-over opportunities, a time in which they all lived other stories, again fully possible stories which they had no inkling of and which they could only come into contact with accidentally in such a momentary intersection of times, like the spontaneous twitching of a nameless nerve which you don't expect to twitch since your brain hasn't sent it a command, and in such cases had she not really jumped from one time into another? But the kiss, real or not, seemed to put an end to everything.

Spartacus seemed crushed, Elena told him that they needed to talk and she dumped him completely cold-bloodedly, we're not going to see each other anymore, she had said, but why, there is no why, because that's how I want it, and Sirma once again felt duped, not to mention guilty and shamefaced, maybe Spartacus really had been in love after all, maybe some part of her had even suspected this, and Elena had played her yet again, by refusing to say why she was leaving, if she had told him Sirma made me, then they would've had a fight and in the fight everything would have come out and been cleared up, now it was pointless for Sirma herself to tell him how she had gone to her, how she had listened to her and listened to her, and how she had felt her kiss on her lips, a conspiratorial sign, a seal of silence. Maya didn't want to talk about her erstwhile best-friend-from-grade-school, and in the end Sirma had no choice but to keep quiet. But she thought up the mysteries to make sure that something like that could never happen again, and perhaps, she said to herself now, also in some desperate attempt to finally experience some satisfaction from that overrated physical exercise, as one of their acquaintances put it, who else to have sex with, if not your friends, and if she hadn't thought up this form, it surely would've happened anyway, but unexpectedly and abruptly, it would have pounced on them unprepared, and perhaps everything would have fallen apart. As for Elena, she disappeared, she must've gone to America, but what really would have happened if they had nevertheless let her into their magic circle, in one of those other times, which intersected with theirs and could you always tell when one time jumped into another, Sirma heard footsteps, human footsteps, scraping along the gravel-strewn path, and heard Spartacus's voice, wasn't it somewhere here, so why don't I see them, because you're blind, she yelled at him from the tree, I'm right here, and explained to them how Elena's father had slinked off.

And the next strange thing: he came back with a guitar. He looked more surprised than they were. How could this have happened to me twice, he said, just look how the story has repeated itself, and it's a nice guitar, so that means you'll play, Maya clapped and Sirma entered the picture she knew Maya was imagining, a beach at night and a guitar in the hands of the likeable man, she even felt like laughing, but the hesitation Krustev wore like a coat again hung on his shoulders, I guess I could play a bit, he said, but I haven't touched a guitar in a long time, in a really long time. Why not, asked Spartacus, and Krustev replied I have no fucking idea.

She dreamed of sand that stuck to her skin, as if she had broken out in a tiny, glittering rash, but that was because she was playing in the sand with her brother, they were little again, and both naked, and she tried not to look at the thing jutting out so ridiculously between his legs, her mother had told her that it wasn't polite to talk about things that were between people's legs and she decided that in that case it surely wasn't polite to think about them either, so she tried to think about the castle they were building together, but the sea washed over it at regular intervals and demolished it, their castle was a failure because the professors didn't want to teach them anything, and while she was thinking this, she was left alone in the castle, naked and ridiculous, well yes, after all her brother had left, hadn't he, she had to figure out this castle on her own, but she could feel how the grains of sand sticking to her body were multiplying and becoming like armor, at one point she looked down and saw that it wasn't sand at all, but tiny flowers, while Maya and Spartacus were standing a little ways off, looking at her and pointing, and yelling something, but she couldn't hear them, what, she yelled in turn, come on, what's wrong, talk louder, they pointed at her, at the castle her legs were straddling, she looked down and saw a baby squirming between her legs, a real baby, but how had she given birth without being pregnant, and then she realized that she hadn't given birth, but precisely the opposite, it was backing up into her, without her even feeling it, and right before the monstrous creature hid inside her and disappeared, she managed to see its face, it may have been a baby, but it had Elena's face.

In the morning she quickly forgot her repugnant dream, but it popped into her mind again as she was waiting for Spartacus to come out of the bathroom so she could go in, too, and again, like on the ship, like so long ago over her bowl of cereal, her stomach suddenly heaved, this time bringing up a stream of black coffee along with the stomach acid, which dribbled down her chin, right at that moment Spartacus opened the door, saw her and jumped, what's the matter with you, are you okay, I'm fine, she said, wiping her chin, did you get yourself nice and clean for tonight, and pinched him on the ass, but after she was left alone in the bathroom and had locked the door, she realized that she had no desire whatsoever for that which awaited them that evening.

But still they went, how could they not go, Spartacus and Maya obediently followed their reluctant leader, yesterday, as they had splashed around in the choppy sea, which was now smooth as a mirror, as far as could be seen in the darkness, it was cloudy and there were no stars, yesterday she had noticed that hill at the edge of the city looming steeply over the water, surely no one goes there at night, she had pointed it out to them then and they had agreed, so now they were climbing the hill off the road that led to the city, looking for a good spot, well, well, said Spartacus behind her back, here we'll have ourselves a nice view of the sea, real box seats, and he laughed, but quickly fell silent, perhaps because Maya had shot him a stern look, they weren't supposed to laugh during the mysteries, laughter pulled them out of the magic of the ritual and revealed its full absurdity, Sirma thought to herself and sat down on the ground. The view really was nice and the wind wasn't blowing like last night. I wonder what Krustev is doing, she asked herself, this is all so stupid, it's surely completely obvious to him what they were up to and now he must be laughing at them for their strict adherence to a timetable to restrain the hormones, in his place Elena would have been going crazy with curiosity, to say nothing of insisting that she be allowed to join in. Breathe, said Maya, having taken up the lotus pose, breathe, doesn't it smell wonderful. It smelled of all sorts of grasses and herbs, a whole symphony of scents, in which it was impossible to distinguish any one aroma. Still sitting in her snobby lotus pose, Maya began fondling her own breasts lightly and Sirma suddenly burst out laughing, the loud giggle burst from her mouth like stomach acid, scattered into the night and startled the scents. Spartacus and Maya looked at her in surprise, she kept laughing, it was like an allergy attack, she couldn't stop herself, her eyes swam with tears, her stomach shook with uncontrollable spasms and the laughter jumped from her throat like gravel, tiny grains of laughter stuck to it and in the end she choked, the laughter passed into coughing, she finally got a hold of herself, but she saw Spartacus and Maya's astonished faces and burst out laughing again, this time only a short, single swath. Spartacus also gave a crooked, bewildered smile, what's the matter, Maya asked, well, nothing's the matter, said Sirma, isn't it funny, she got up and said, come on, enough of this ridiculousness, let's go, but what about the mysteries, Spartacus asked, confused, what about the mysteries, Sirma mimicked him, if you're all hung up on a fuck, well fine then, if you've already gotten it up, we'll help you out. That's ridiculous, Spartacus said, offended, isn't that exactly what I'm telling you, it's ridiculous, Sirma replied and remained standing as they kept sitting on the grass foolishly, silent for some time, then Maya said so it's all over? I don't know what it all is, Sirma said, but I think something's over, only I don't quite know what yet. But still, said Maya, it really does smell good. Spartacus got up; and what will we do now? What else, said Sirma, we'll go find the Big Boss. On the way down, she heard Spartacus start snickering, followed by Maya, she started laughing, too, and the three of them came down the hill like a scree of laughter.

But when they reached the apartment after a half-hour of fast walking and one or two wrong turns in the old town, Krustev was gone and the only sound in the house was the monotonous and unintelligible buzzing of the TV in the landlady's room. Sirma couldn't imagine Krustev keeping the desiccated old woman with the aquiline nose company in front of the TV, but she still held her ear to the door and listened for the sound of a second person. She shook her head. He took the guitar, Maya noted. Nothing else was missing. Hmm, Spartacus put in, I wonder if he decided to take off just like that in the car again, actually he would have every right to do that, Sirma added, but I doubt it, I say we look for him on the beach. As they made their way out of the old town and set off on the coastal road along the harbor, which was piled with the overripe fruit of yachts and tourist boats, she asked herself why they were even looking for him, but they didn't have anything else to do in any case and certainly none of them felt like going to bed just now, so the three of them continued quickly striding along the sea, it was still cloudy and when they reached the zone where the hotels were not yet completely full, a few of them hadn't even opened yet, beyond the bright circles of the street lamps you couldn't see much of anything. And so they had almost made it back to the hill they had come down earlier and surely they were all thinking it, but no one said it aloud. They took the last sets of stairs from the road down to the beach, took off their shoes and set out over the coarse brown sand. He might not even be on the beach at all, Maya said, he might not be, Sirma agreed, but then again he might, it depends on which time we're in, which time, Maya was confused, never mind, she replied, it doesn't matter. The sea murmured pleasantly and its black mass rocked slightly, in the dark it looked like a huge, living, gentle monster. Here at the very end of the beach, there were no umbrellas or chaise longues, in fact, there wasn't anything, but right when she was telling herself there's nothing here, Spartacus suddenly said what's that? In the darkness, which was disconcerted by the distant lights, they could make out some lump in the sand, they headed towards it and finally saw that it was the guitar, with jeans, a shirt and a beach towel carefully set on top of it. Fuck, Sirma said and suddenly felt afraid, fear hit her like a punch to the stomach, she felt herself dissolving into the surrounding darkness and collapsing to the ground like a handful of sand. Spartacus and Maya were already getting undressed in feverish silence, she followed their example, but never before had her fingers unbuttoned her clothes so clumsily, she found herself in some terrible slow time, which trickled like rough sand from the globe of an hourglass, and she wanted to say something, she wanted to curse Krustev and his flippant whim to go into the sea alone at night when he couldn't swim, then she was seized with the total certainty that he had gone in to drown himself, fucking Mr. Depressed, to drown himself in the sea and to slip away from everything, from his dead wife and his distant daughter, the sight of his bloated body floating all too calmly on the waves hit her right in the eye, the drowned Herr Burgher, a luxury-loving corpse, a lump of death upon the funereal dance of the sea. Spartacus and Maya were already running down the beach, racing into the water and quickly swimming out, growing distant, and she followed them, going in a little to one side so they would be spread out in their search for him, perhaps he was still alive, perhaps they would find him in the darkness, drag him out by his seaweed-tangled hair and pump his stomach until he spit out all the black water he had swallowed, but it was dark, fiendishly dark, the fucking clouds hadn't budged; and without stars and the moon, with only the city lights reflecting on the black sea, a greasy semi-darkness spread, in which she could no longer even see Spartacus and Maya's heads, but she suddenly saw something next to her, she jumped, screamed and Krustev's voice, offensively alive, said, well now, fancy meeting you here. You're here, she shouted, well, yes, said Krustev, adding proudly, I was swimming. She felt like kissing him and slapping him, a mother to this man twice her age, she tried to call to the other two, but a sudden wave filled her mouth with water and as she spit angrily, Krustev, who had remained on the surface, yelled out loudly, hey, I'm over here, and they soon saw Spartacus and Maya's heads swimming towards them from different directions.

As they came out of the water together, Sirma was still shaking from fury and relief, even though, she told herself, the three of them were not supposed to be here at all, and if everything had gone according to plan they wouldn't be here, then this whole scene would never have happened, but in that case every moment and every action gave rise to and at the same time ruled out countless possibilities, tiny grains of sand, indistinguishable from one another they all dried off with the same towel which Krustev had prudently brought along, how had the thought that he would go and drown himself ever crossed her mind, given that the man had brought a towel, and they sat down on the ground. You brought the guitar, said Spartacus. Yes, said Krustev, I brought it, yes, and he drummed his fingers on the body, scattering the brief buzzing of the strings in the air. He finally made up his mind, picked up the guitar, put it on his lap and tested the strings, sighed, and started playing some melody, Sirma didn't know it, maybe Spartacus did, given his obsession with rock music and his ability to fish out all sorts of things that had been crammed helter-skelter into the depths of his memory, she looked at him, but he didn't respond, he was just listening and watching Krustev's hands, the melody was nice, lively, and somehow charmingly infantile, it crumbled out from under his fingers and settled crystallized onto the sand, and when it was done, Krustev laughed and carefully set down the guitar. What was that, Spartacus asked, there was no way you'd know it, he replied, an old melody of mine that never made it into a song, I wrote it when Elena was born. Sirma jumped, suddenly jerked back to her repugnant dream from the previous night, but the image of the monstrous baby shoving its way inside her immediately scattered into the air and Krustev's melody returned, completely ordinary, such a soothing ordinary melody, she called me tonight, Krustev added. She did? Sirma felt a coldness in her teeth. She decided to come home without telling me, Krustev explained, and when she didn't find me there, naturally she called. So that's it, said Sirma, Krustev seemed to drift off somewhere, but he soon started talking again, I remember, he began, I remember how once she got lost as a little girl, at a market, her mother and I were out of our heads with worry, we turned the whole market upside down, it was awful, I've never been so scared in my whole life, but in the end we found her; and where did we find her, on a side street, sitting and watching some boys fighting, I couldn't believe it, they were just kids, eleven or twelve years old, wailing away with their fists, two boys were beating a third, they pushed him down to the ground, they were kicking him, it's like a black-and-white movie in my memory, them kicking the boy on the ground, and Elena, just a little girl, was sitting on the curb, watching them and smiling, she was entranced, I yelled at them, only then did they see me and run away, and the boy they were beating up, I wanted to help him, but he jumped up and ran off, too, while Elena was just sitting there smiling. They hung there in awkward silence, like wet laundry on a clothes line. So, he said finally, you want to head back tomorrow? Spartacus coughed. Yes, said Sirma, and it was as if the whole sea burst into her and filled her when she repeated yes.

In the house the walls are sleeping, the rugs are sleeping, the television is sleeping, the switched-off presence of sounds and images. The lamps are sleeping, bat-like bracket lamps and quiet ceiling lights, loudly snoring chandeliers. Krustev is sleeping, hung on the wall, his wife is sleeping on one side of him, his daughter on the other, they are sleeping with open eyes, smiling amid the lawn outside. The half-empty bottle of expensive whiskey taken out of the liquor cabinet with the magnetic door is sleeping.

But in the garden all times are awake at once, the leafy clocks of the birches spin around like mad, the grass bends uneasily, along the fence ants scuttle, headed every which way, they touch antennae, disappear into the dirt and come above again, and there in the unmowed lawn, where the family portrait was taken five years ago, now amid the unwitnessed licentiousness, the only person nearby lies sleeping, Elena is sleeping on the lawn and inside her names and stories spin, and in one of those simultaneously possible wakeful times, in the quiet and carefully stored time of shame, right at that moment she opens her eyes.

Angel Igov is a Bulgarian writer, literary critic, and translator. He has published two collections of short stories, and his first collection won the Southern Spring award for debuts in fiction. Igov has also translated books by Paul Auster, Martin Amis, Angela Carter, and Ian McEwan into Bulgarian. He is currently getting his PhD in European Literature.

Angela Rodel is the translator of *The Apocalypse Comes at 6 P.M.* by Georgi Gospodinov, *Party Headquarters* by Georgi Tenev, *Thrown into Nature* by Milen Ruskov, and *18% Gray* by Zachary Karabashliev. She was awarded a 2010 PEN Translation Fund Grant for her translation of several stories from Tenev's *Holy Light*.

Open Letter—the University of Rochester's nonprofit, literary translation press—is one of only a handful of publishing houses dedicated to increasing access to world literature for English readers. Publishing ten titles in translation each year, Open Letter searches for works that are extraordinary and influential, works that we hope will become the classics of tomorrow.

Making world literature available in English is crucial to opening our cultural borders, and its availability plays a vital role in maintaining a healthy and vibrant book culture. Open Letter strives to cultivate an audience for these works by helping readers discover imaginative, stunning works of fiction and poetry, and by creating a constellation of international writing that is engaging, stimulating, and enduring.

Current and forthcoming titles from Open Letter include works from Argentina, Denmark, France, Germany, Latvia, Netherlands, Poland, Russia, and many other countries.

www.openletterbooks.org